HAWAI'I'S BEST
spOOky
TALES

TRUE

LOCAL

SPINE-TINGLERS

COLLECTED BY
RICK CARROLL

THE
BESS
PRESS

3565 HARDING AVENUE, HONOLULU, HAWAI'I 96816

Design and maps: Carol Colbath
Moon logo from a design by Kevin Hand

Library of Congress Cataloging in Publication Data

Carroll, Rick
    Hawaii's best spooky tales : true local
spine-tinglers / collected by Rick Carroll.
        p.   cm.
    Includes illustrations.
    ISBN 1-57306-031-3
    1. Ghost stories, American – Hawaii.
2. Tales – Hawaii. 3. Legends – Hawaii.
I. Title.
GR580.H3.C371 1997   398.25-dc20

Printed in the United States of America

ISBN 1-57306-031-3

For my father, Virgil Max Carroll
March 6, 1920 - March 24, 1997

About Rick Carroll

Author and travel writer Rick Carroll is a former daily journalist for the *San Francisco Chronicle* who covered Hawai'i and the Pacific for United Press International.

Carroll has written six Hawai'i guidebooks, including *Great Outdoor Adventures of Hawaii*. His next book, *Travelers Tales Hawaii*, an anthology of personal discoveries in the Hawaiian Islands, is due in 1998. He is now working on a cultural guide to the South Pacific island of Huahine with Dr. Yosihiko Sinoto of the Bishop Museum.

His illustrated articles on Rapa Nui (Easter Island) and French Polynesia have won the Lowell Thomas Award of the Society of American Travel Writers and the Gold Award of Pacific Asia Travel Association. His reports from the Philippines during the Marcos era won a National Headliner's Award.

Hawai'i's Best Spooky Tales is Carroll's second collection of true accounts of inexplicable encounters in the Islands.

Carroll lives in Hawai'i and Friday Harbor, Washington.

Acknowledgments

"English," wrote Virginia Woolf, "which can express the thoughts of Hamlet and the tragedy of Lear, has no words for the shiver or the headache . . . ."

Her thoughts come to mind now because in the creation of this book I found many words for both shiver and headache, usually around midnight. The second time around is supposed to be easier, but it's not.

Creating anthologies is like juggling blindfolded. In the end, somehow, everything falls into place and a book emerges, but not without the work of many who too often go unrecognized.

To those who helped make this collection of true spooky stories a reality I say thank you:

Benjamin Bess, for his idealism and perseverance; editor Revé Shapard, who shared the shiver and the headache; Carol Colbath, for her spooky cover and book design; and everyone else at The Bess Press, for their support: Pam Soderberg, Jeela Ongley, Alison Rowland-Ciszek, Lori Bodine, Robin Canape, and Mike Okawa; Mark Bernstein for his artful legal counsel.

Every contributing author, especially Gordon Morse of Volcano, Kaui Goring Philpotts on Maui, Catherine Chandler on the Big Island, and Eugene Le Beaux at sea aboard the SS *Independence*.

Teachers and librarians, especially Sandy Martino at Maui Community College, Margaret Grady at Lahaina Intermediate, and school librarians Nancy Schildt, of Lanikai School, and Joanne Haynes, of Maunawili School.

Special thanks to Nanette Napoleon Purnell of The Cemetery Project for her continued support, Brad Adams of Antiques-Windward, for his revelations in "The Secret Life of Things."

To each and all of you, mahalo and, please, be careful out there.

Table of Contents

Introduction

If you go out after dark in Hawai'i, you must be careful. They are out there. Watching. You almost always feel their presence. Sometimes, you may even see them. Night marchers still walk ancient paths to conduct rituals and ceremonies. *Kāhuna* talk to rocks and the rocks talk back. You can be "prayed" to death. More than a century and a half after the demise of idolatry and human sacrifice, Hawai'i is alive with mystery. Secret caves contain old canoes and feathered capes of long-dead *ali'i*. The Bishop Museum has the world's greatest collection of fishhooks made of the bones of defeated warriors.

Places are still *kapu*. There are signs to heed, rules to obey. Or else. Inexplicable things happen. Houses shake. Bulldozers fly. Cars leave the road. Freeways collapse. If you think, as I once did, that Hawai'i is just another warm, fuzzy place popular with newlyweds and TV game show prize winners, think again. Hawai'i is full of places of power, and mystery, and supernatural events that make you shiver in the tropic heat. Every island is so alive with ancestral spirits it gives me chicken skin. (That's the local pidgin expression for goose bumps.)

Give Voice to the People

People in Hawai'i like to tell about their encounters with mysterious forces—it's part of Polynesia's rich oral tradition—but until now few have had the opportunity to see their stories come to life in print, preserved for others to enjoy.

For nearly two decades, as a journalist, author, and travel writer, it has been my practice to include "the voice of Hawai'i" in every article or book I wrote, but that was never enough. I wanted to read what I heard every day in

Hawai'i—the unique patois of pidgin, the easy, honest Island-style of storytelling that you sometimes still hear at backyard *lū'au*; I wanted somehow to gather up all the small but important stories handed down from one generation to the next and press them between covers like old flower *lei*. It became my goal to encourage new, local writers and usher them into print, since only by hearing the voice of the people can anyone, *kama'āina* or *malihini*, hope to gain a true sense of the place.

That goal is realized in *Hawai'i's Best Spooky Tales: True Local Spine-Tinglers*. This collection includes contributions from thirty-seven authors, most of them previously unpublished. One of those stories is "Great-Grandpa's Ghost," by Jerrica Ann Keanuhea Lum, now a fifth-grade student at O'ahu's Maunawili School, who is one of Hawai'i's youngest published authors.

Three other stories in this anthology are by schoolchildren, students of Margaret Grady, an enterprising Lahaina Intermediate School teacher who asked her students to write their own first-person stories. "Our entire class," Mrs. Grady told me, "was taken along the path of the writing process while writing about a subject they certainly all enjoy." Published here are "The Glowing Lady," by Micah Curimao, "The Sandalwood Warrior," by Asheley Kahahane, and "The Ghost Who Surfs," by Hapa Koloi.

In addition to these children, the other contributing authors are an amazing cross-section of otherwise ordinary people who have experienced the extraordinary in Hawai'i: they are young adults, baby boomers, and retirees, from six islands and several mainland states, including California, Arizona, and North Carolina; they include public school teachers, professional musicians, writers, and artists, a library employee, a judicial clerk, a teacher of Japanese, a medical technologist, a professional windsurfer, a mechanic, a store manager and a sales rep, and several Ph.D.'s.

My friend Lei-Ann Stender Durant, herself the author of a story about a spooky experience, calls people who are sensitive to the supernatural "feelers," a term I like although it may suggest that only a few special people are permitted to experience the inexplicable. We all know it can happen to anyone, anytime, especially in Hawai'i. And those who doubt the possibility, those who say, "I don't believe in all that stuff," are usually the most susceptible. In the end, we are all "feelers."

New Voices and Strange Encounters

For easy reading, *Hawai'i's Best Spooky Tales* is divided into ten sections whose headings give a clue to what lies ahead. As you soon shall see, these stories are not twice-told campfire tales, or local legends about carrying pork over the Pali (everyone in Hawai'i knows all about that), but new contemporary tales of supernatural events actually experienced by real people.

These are just a few of the authentic episodes you will encounter in *Hawai'i's Best Spooky Tales*:

- A night at the beach and a trip to a favorite fishing spot turn into nightmares.
- A fish-shaped 'aumakua stone found on Kaua'i after Hurricane 'Iniki causes splitting headaches.
- A sudden gust of wind douses a campfire on the slopes of Mauna Kea when a skeptic derides Madame Pele.
- A pen floats in mid-air in a haunted Honolulu apartment house.
- A young surfer on Maui discovers he is not alone on the waves of Kapalua.
- A tree speaks Hawaiian at the entrance to the Royal Mausoleum in Nu'uanu.

- The bones of a child in sand dunes near Maui's Ho'okipa Beach may help save a life.

What we have here, then, is not just another book about ghosts. While ghostly figures are central to some stories ("The Stone," "Jason's House," "North Shore Spirits," "Fading Figures," "Woman in White," "Hickam Ghosts," "Mamoru," "The Ghost Who Surfs," "Great-Grandpa's Ghost," and "The Ghost Fleet of Kamehameha I") others feature animism, primal fears, old and new taboos, or *kapu*, as we say in the Islands, and elements of nature—the sky, sea, and earth—with a little myth and legend to keep it all in context.

These are the stories of old and new Hawai'i told by many people in many voices from many points of view. The result is a book rich in texture and complex in spirit, like Hawai'i itself.

If you, like me, browse a book instead of reading it from cover to cover, I direct you immediately to four stories that surely will become classics of Hawai'i literature.

- George Fujita's "Mu'umu'u" is a story richly human in its recalling of the simple terrors of small-kid time. It gave me chills, made me laugh, and really took me back to old Maui in those not so very faraway days. An excellent and scary Hawai'i story, "Mu'umu'u" will delight everyone who reads it. Who doesn't still practice "side eye"?
- Helen Fujie's trilogy—"Roy and Pele," "Katsup," and "Cowboy Kauwenaole"—offers delicious insights into plantation days on a remote tropical island. The scent of lavender that leads to a Victorian bedroom in a cave below the Garden of Gods on the Island of Lāna'i haunts me now.
- Kaui Philpotts' story about "The Saltbox House" reveals

an eerie link with a distant relative in far-off Nantucket, Massachusetts.

• And who won't get a shiver when they read Tania Leslie and Rich Asprec's "Night Games," set in the old gymnasium at Konawaena High School on the Big Island of Hawai'i.

You should probably avoid reading any of the stories just before bedtime. Nightmares, you know.

Historic Chillers

Three of the true spooky tales are historic chillers. The oldest, "The Ghost Fleet of Kamehameha I," translated by Mary Kawena Pukui, dates back to 1864. I discovered the story in a yellowed old manuscript entitled "Seeing Thousands of Ghosts for a Single Night in Leilono, Hawai'i" one afternoon by accident while searching the Bishop Museum archives. Leilono, incidentally, is the old name for Moanalua on O'ahu, which apparently was haunted more than a century ago.

"The Poi Pounder," by the late, great author and raconteur Ed Sheehan, is excerpted from *The Hawaiians*, by Robert Goodman, Ed Sheehan, and Gavan Daws. Big Island author Gordon Morse's "Pele" is a local classic that recounts how he and two others met the Hawaiian fire goddess in broad daylight.

And, finally, there is one story handed down through generations that's in a class by itself and should not be overlooked. "*Hitodama*," by Gladys Kaneshige Nakahara, may not be as chilling as it is reverent, but it is no less important. "This is a true story," Mrs. Nakahara told me, "experienced by my paternal grandfather, Sanzuchi Kaneshige, and told to me when I was still small by my father, Kiyomi Kaneshige. It is in honor of my late grandfather's memory that I have decided to record this event for posterity.

"Regardless of whether one believes in the verity of this story, it is nevertheless a Hawaiian legacy which, I feel, should be perpetually passed down to the younger generations. Stories such as this make us aware that it is Hawai'i's history, built largely on the contributions and sacrifice of early immigrants, that makes Hawai'i such a unique and profoundly interesting place."

Her story and all the others in *Hawai'i's Best Spooky Tales* make it required reading for anyone who hopes to understand the supernatural side of Hawai'i. I know the stories will give you a shiver, especially if you read them at home, alone.

And for those of you brave enough to venture out in search of chills, I have added a scary little bonus—the first Guide to Spooky Places, which directs you to actual places most likely to make your skin crawl.

The Guide to Spooky Places

In the heart of Honolulu, an otherwise modern and sophisticated American city of 800,000 souls, you can find on the grounds of 'Iolani Palace a heaping mound of earth that looks like a makeshift grave. There is no physical proof that any royal body yet reposes there, but the site is considered sacred and thus *kapu* by prior association. On the Big Island of Hawai'i, out on the Great Ka'ū Desert, there are footsteps frozen in lava. A *heiau* on Moloka'i, which served as a kind of university of Polynesian voodoo, has *mana* strong enough to lean on.

Seldom if ever mentioned in guidebooks or glossy travel magazines (the visitors' bureau obviously doesn't want to scare you away), all these places have one thing in common: they produce that delicious shiver everyone in Hawai'i calls "chicken skin."

Pele

I have met a number of people, otherwise ordinary, god-fearing people, Hawaiians and *haole* alike, who claim they have seen Madame Pele, the goddess of Hawaiian volcanoes. Of all the Pele stories I have heard, this is my favorite because it involves four eyewitnesses—a journalist, a pilot, a volcanologist, and a sugar planter—who each saw Pele in broad daylight.

Pele

The day we met Pele we were not supposed to meet anyone. Please note the "we." There were three witnesses to this story of meeting the fiery goddess of Hawai'i volcanoes. I wouldn't dare tell you about this if I had been alone.

My friends were a pilot, a scientist, and a sugar plantation manager.

Our visit with Pele was in the spring of 1955. The goddess was island building down in the lower Puna area on the flank of Kīlauea Volcano. It was the first eruption in modern history to happen in a populated area.

For over a week a large section of Puna had been cut off from the rest of the island by two rivers of molten lava as they raced from the vents into the ocean. Residents of the area were now refugees in a school gymnasium in the sugar town of Pāhoa.

The manager of the Puna Sugar Company wanted to inspect what was left of his fields in the abandoned area. He talked the pilot of a small plane into landing on a cinder road between the lava flows so he could inspect the area on foot.

Since there were two empty seats in the airplane, a volcano scientist was invited to go along. I was talked into going to record the trip with camera and pen as I was a newsman in those days.

The pilot landed the Cessna aircraft on the road. The landing distance was so short he had to stand on the brakes to keep from going into the bushes.

The four of us walked around inspecting the sugar fields, a path of bananas, and a sweet potato farm plot. There were no houses in this section.

Imagine our surprise when we came upon a Lady sitting at the edge of a sugar field.

Later I checked my notes and I definitely wrote her down as a Lady. That's the impression I had. In my estimation, a girl would have been under twenty. She was older, but not by much.

If it were a woman, the person would have showed more maturity in dress and hairdo, and a certain domestication of mannerisms. You know, she would have had that look that sends children to bed without a fuss at eight p.m.

But a Lady has the charm of sophistication. She carries herself with authority even when sitting. She has soft features, clearness of skin, a sculpturing of the nose that denotes breeding. This Lady sitting by the side of the path had all of these at first glance.

She wore a red *mu'umu'u* with black markings that resembled bamboo. She displayed no jewelry. A cloud of jet black hair flowed behind her shoulders and down to the middle of her back. She was barefoot.

"Hi," said the manager, recovering from his surprise.

"Aloha," she answered.

To this day I cannot truthfully explain how that "aloha" sounded. Something like a lover saying it to his love in the moonlight with the sound of the sea whispering on sands would be a fair attempt.

"What are you doing here?" asked the sugar planter in an authoritative voice. After all, he owned this land.

"Just resting in the shade of the sugarcane," the lady replied, giving us a radiant smile.

"No one is supposed to be in this area," the scientist said. "The National Guard evacuated everyone a week ago. Why did you stay behind? You know you're trapped in between lava flows here."

The Lady's smile just grew wider as if that were answer enough.

"What's your name?" I inquired, poising a pencil over my notebook.

She said something very musical in Hawaiian that sounded to me like the name of a fern. I wrote it down phonetically, and it appears as "u'ulei" in my notes. (Later, I looked the word up in a Hawaiian dictionary. It's actually *'ūlei*, a Hawai'i shrub with small white rose-like flowers.)

The pilot frowned and turned to us. "I could make two trips in the plane and take her out," he said.

"Oh, I won't leave here," the Lady said. "At least not today. I have work to do. Perhaps I'll be ready to go somewhere else next week."

"Well, if you don't want to come away with us now, you may have to later today or tomorrow," the scientist said. "We'll have to report you to Civil Defense and they will send a helicopter in for you. The eruption has caused an emergency in this part of the island, and there are laws to protect people."

"I follow my own laws," the Lady said, and for the first time she stopped smiling.

I remember looking into her eyes at that moment and what I saw was familiar. While in college, I had spent a Christmas vacation with some friends in a home on a frozen lake in Wisconsin. We all slept in the living room because the cast iron stove could only heat that room. The stove was loaded with wood at bedtime, but by dawn it was freezing to the touch. However, when I lifted the lid to put in more wood, there were two gleaming cherry-red coals nestling in the gray ashes that promised instant rekindling.

The Lady's features were now cold, and those same two glowing coals were deep within her gray eyes.

Perhaps my three companions had somewhat the same feeling, because the manager said, "We'll finish our inspection of this area, and if you want to go out with us, you can wait by the plane." He gestured up the road toward where we landed.

We continued walking. But for some strange reason, we had only gone ten feet or so when the idea that this might be Pele entered our minds simultaneously. We turned around to again look at the Lady.

She was gone!

We ran back. The manager plunged into the cane field. The pilot went up the road. The scientist jogged down another path. I stood and called her name. We didn't find her.

A spooky feeling began to creep into all of us, like a cloud invading a rain forest at dusk.

"I think it's time to go," the pilot said.

No one disagreed.

We got into the plane and taxied to the end of the cinder road. The pilot gunned the engine and stood on the brakes. When he released the brakes, we lurched forward. Halfway down the road it was obvious the plane was too heavily loaded to clear the trees ahead. Landing on a small road was one thing. Taking off with a heavy load was another.

We stopped.

"Someone has to get out," the pilot said. "I'll come back for you later."

The "you" was directed at me. I was sitting next to the door. For reasons not entirely clear to me, I made no protest and got out of the plane.

I was scared. I did not want to socialize with anyone, especially a Lady. And as the plane took off, diminished to a dot, then disappeared, I fervently wished I was somewhere else. Anywhere else would do.

My thoughts were of Pele sightings I had read. They were

usually about seeing an old woman, or a pretty young one, during an eruption.

The common one is that she is hitchhiking, gets into a car, asks for a cigarette, lights it with the tip of her finger, and then, when the driver momentarily looks the other way, she disappears.

Another story is that she comes to a house accompanied by a white dog and asks for something to eat or drink. When given something, she goes on her way. But if she is refused, she stamps her foot, and very soon a finger of molten lava branches off from the main flow and destroys the house.

An hour dragged by, and when no Lady appeared, I began to laugh at myself. That wasn't Pele. She was probably a resident who had decided to stay in the area to take care of her cat or dog. I had a name and description.

I would solve this mystery once I got out.

The pilot did return, and an hour later I walked into Civil Defense headquarters at the refugee gym. The pilot, the scientist, and the sugar planter were there. The four of us grilled the residents of Puna. The Lady's name and description didn't fit anyone they knew. The National Guard commander and Civil Defense workers all assured us they had done a thorough job in getting everyone out—people and their pets.

Hawai'i-born author and former *Honolulu Advertiser* reporter Gordon Morse lives in Volcano, the village near the entrance to Hawai'i Volcanoes National Park, home of Madame Pele.

On the way home to Lahaina one night, Aunty Emma encounters a hitchhiking woman with a raspy voice who glows in the dark and disappears like mist.

The Glowing Lady

One dark black night, a big lady named Aunty Emma was driving back home from Kahului to Lahaina with the moon shining on her car. She took a fast glance at the side of the road. She saw a lady. The lady was glowing like a reflector.

Aunty Emma stepped on her brakes gently until she stopped. The glowing lady started to jog to the car. When the lady reached the big white van, Aunty Emma said, "Come, come sit in the front."

"I'll sit in the back seat," the lady said in a raspy voice. She opened the door and slammed it shut tight.

Aunty Emma is a talkative person. She brought up a subject about babies. They started talking, but the lady did not talk as much. Aunty Emma asked the lady if she had any babies but she didn't say anything. Aunty Emma was a bit scared. She looked in the back and the lady disappeared like mist.

The next day Aunty Emma had good luck. I think Aunty Emma knew the lady was Pele.

The moral of the story is if you see a person on the side of the road pick them up so you won't get bad luck.

Micah Curimao, age twelve, enjoys writing or telling scary stories because he likes to see the reaction of others. He gains his storytelling ability from his father, Matthew, a source of many legends from around the world. Micah, who lives in Lahaina with his parents, one sister, and a brother, enjoys outdoor activities such as in-line skating, bodyboarding, and paddling canoe.

Three nights before Lisa Okada's wedding on July 5, 1975, a woman with long black hair in a red *muʻumuʻu* appears before Lisa's fiancé on Hilo's Aliʻi Drive. On her wedding night, Lisa receives a most unusual gift from . . .

The Long-Haired Maiden

Anyone born and growing up on the Big Island of Hawai'i has either heard of or experienced the existence of Madame Pele, the Fire Goddess of the Hawai'i Volcanoes National Park. She is seen by residents in her chosen shape or form three or four days before an eruption.

The chicken skin story I am about to share happened in 1975, the year my husband, Neal, and I got married. My maid of honor, Alice, was from Canada, and Neal's best man, John, was from San Francisco. A week prior to our wedding, while playing tour guide and touring the Hawai'i Volcanoes National Park with our out-of-town guests, we were overlooking the Kīlauea crater on an unusually windy day. It was so windy that as Alice stooped to see the crater, her near-waist-length hair swooped upward, rising above her head. We all laughed as she grabbed hold of her hair. For some reason, Neal then predicted that the volcano was going to erupt on our wedding night.

On a Wednesday evening, three nights before our wedding, Neal and his best man, John, were bar-hopping from one hotel to the next on Ali'i Drive. Precisely at 11:55 p.m., as they drove around a bend on the stretch between Kailua-Kona and Keauhou, they saw a maiden with long, black hair, dressed in a black and red *mu'umu'u*, walking in front of their car.

No street lights existed in that remote area of Ali'i Drive. The maiden appeared to be walking in the middle of the road, away from the vehicle, with her back in view. But her feet were nowhere in sight. It was as if she was floating gracefully just above the road.

Neal felt the hair on the back of his neck start to rise, so he slowly, carefully drove around her and passed her. John, a *haole malihini*, unaware of the stories of Madam Pele, said, "Let's stop and pick her up!" Neal, as calmly as he could, said, "Don't turn around; don't even look at her, and I will explain why when we get to the next bar."

After a drink or two, Neal explained to John that the maiden on the road was Pele. John, who was unfamiliar with Hawaiian legends, asked, "Who's Pele?" Neal explained that Pele is the Fire Goddess, who almost always is seen by people several days before an eruption. John asked why Neal didn't try to pick her up, and Neal told him, "Because she did not ask for a ride."

Three nights later, on our wedding night, at precisely 11:55 p.m., July 5, 1975, Mauna Loa, after approximately twenty-five years of rest, erupted. This story of Madam Pele's sighting was not mentioned to me or to anyone else until the evening of our wedding night.

Lisa Okada was born and grew up on the slopes of Mauna Loa in the area of Captain Cook called Nāpōʻopoʻo. "As children in the late 1950s through 1960s," she says, "we had and still maintain high respect for the island from the shores of the Kona Coast to the peaks of Mauna Kea, Mauna Loa, Hualālai, and the Kohala mountains." Lisa would like to dedicate this story—one of many she has heard and told—to all the residents of Kona who labored to make life better for their children.

Kīlauea Volcano

On the Big Island, where Kīlauea volcano daily explodes in red-hot blasts of lava, it is so easy to believe in Pele, the Hawaiian goddess of fire.

Even skeptics stand in awe at the raw fury of a live volcano. Many Native Hawaiians still worship Pele. They bring her offerings, often pints of gin—and for good reason.

Since January 3, 1983, Madame Pele, as believers call her, has claimed two hundred homes and added a huge chunk of land to Hawai'i's charcoal coast. Madame Pele dances nightly on the east rift zone of Hawai'i Volcanoes National Park. Check out her fireworks and you'll believe. You may even see her.

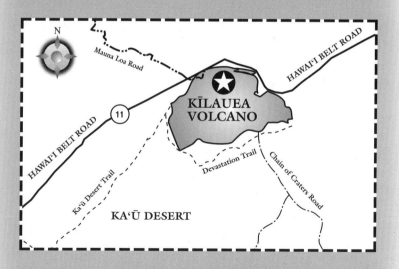

Instead of flying about on her own, Madame Pele sometimes commutes to her fiery tasks in jets and taxicabs, according to Lana T. Paiva, who in 1986, saw the . . .

Lady in Red

Have you ever heard about the Lady in Red? I have—many times as a young girl growing up on the Big Island. My older sister, Hazel, worked at Hertz car rental. She would tell me the volcano would soon erupt because the Lady in Red was seen arriving at the Hilo Airport via Hawaiian Airlines and hailing a cab to take that beautiful drive to the Hawai'i Volcanoes National Park to pay her respects to Madame Pele. I'd never seen her—until 1986.

One beautiful afternoon, my husband, Wendell, and I decided to take a ride up to the Park. I had packed a picnic dinner of musubi, fried chicken, egg roll, vienna sausage, and kim chee. At around 6:00 p.m., as we were cruising along the Chain of Craters Road, we decided to park along the Nāpau Crater. We were alone, enjoying the cool, crisp, gentle breezes, ready to eat our dinner, when a taxi drove up and parked in front of us. Who do you think got out? It was the Lady in Red!

She strolled across the parking lot, crossed the Chain of Craters Road, and stood at the foot of a row of old spatter cones. No visible steam rose from any of the cones. The Lady in Red chanted in Hawaiian and tossed in some coins. The vents roared to life with steam!

As the taxi driver waited to take her to her next destination, Wendell and I looked at each other in disbelief. We decided to leave the area immediately! Would the earth start to tremble?

Would the road split open and make it impossible for us to leave? Where did the Lady in Red come from? Where did she go? Who was she? We still don't know.

Lana T. Paiva is a Judicial Clerk with the Family Court, Third Circuit, in Hilo. Born in Laupāhoehoe on the Big Island, she graduated from Hilo High School and attended the Hawaiʻi Community College. She and her husband, Wendell D. Paiva, have two children.

Footprints in Ash

Out in the great Ka'ū Desert on the road to Hawai'i
Volcanoes National Park you pass layer upon layer of
lava flows. Only those in recent history are record-
ed—1790, 1880, 1920, 1926, 1950, 1969, 1971,
1974. The dates draw closer in time the deeper you
go into the desert, crossing The Great Crack and the
Southwest Rift Zone, onward to Kīlauea volcano,
which created all this desert, this island.

Along Ka'ū Desert Trail are footprints in hard-
ened ash. Whose are they? Flashback to 1790. King
Kamehameha wages war to gain control of Hawai'i.
Opposing forces led by Keoua attempt to cross the
desert. Kīlauea volcano erupts, kills eighty warriors.
Dead in their tracks. Keoua surrenders to
Kamehameha and is sacrificed. It's something to think
about as you drive across the scorched Ka'ū Desert
toward still-bubbling Kīlauea volcano, which to this
day influences landscape and history.

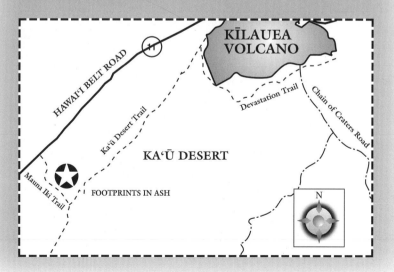

Although few people ever see Madame Pele, Roy Fujie has had three amazing encounters with the elusive fire goddess, twice on Lāna'i in the 1940s, and again in the late 1950s on the Big Island of Hawai'i, where she thanked him for a cigarette in her own volatile way.

Roy and Pele

In the early 1940s, Pele was seen on Lāna'i by my husband, Roy Fujie. She was all in white and rode on a fiery horse with her white dog running beside it. She came down Ninth Avenue from the Hotel Lāna'i area, crossed Lāna'i Avenue and headed toward Fraser Avenue and the Catholic Church.

Roy heard the clippity-clop of the horse's hooves, but the horse with Pele and her dog seemed to fly or float through the air.

He had just finished his night shift at the power house there, so he thought he was just imagining all this in the early morning moonlight.

In the late 1950s, Roy was the night shift supervisor (*luna*) for the pineapple pickers in the farthest fields to the southwest of Lāna'i plantation when Pele again appeared. She was all in white, a little old lady with her white dog on the dirt road. Roy stopped his pick-up truck to offer her a ride, but she only asked for a cigarette. So he reached into his glove compartment and got a fresh new cigarette and lit it with his own to give it to her. But she wasn't there when he offered it to her.

When there was a radio news report about the rumblings of an imminent eruption at Kīlauea Volcano, Roy went to visit his two brothers in Hilo and went to Halema'uma'u crater. There was a boatload of tourists off the *Lurline* that morning at 9:30.

They were all very disappointed because nothing was happening.

So Roy took a fresh cigarette from his shirt pocket, lit it and threw it into the caldera saying, "Here, Pele, you did not take the cigarette I offered you on Lāna'i, so now please puff on this today."

Then in full confidence he told the tourists around him that Pele would surely erupt that night. To his great joy and luck, Pele did blow up that very evening at 9:30. The *Lurline* crowd came back to thank Roy, whom they recognized as the fellow in a *lau hala* hat with a *kolohala* feather lei who had offered Pele a cigarette and asked her to puff that day.

A retired school teacher and administrator, Helen Fujie writes regularly for the *Lanai Times* and occasionally for the *Honolulu Advertiser*. Born and raised in Kahului, Maui, she is a graduate of the University of Hawai'i College of Education. She taught on Lāna'i for forty years and worked as a substitute teacher and volunteer until 1996. Married to Roy K. Fujie since 1944, she and her husband have three sons and two granddaughters. "Roy and Pele" is from a collection, "Lāna'i Visions," which was awarded an Honorable Mention in the 1997 story competition.

Stones and Bones

When a Hoʻokipa windsurfer runs aground on a deserted Maui beach, he finds not only the bones of a baby long buried in the sand dunes but a carved Hawaiian fishhook that magically saves the life of a child.

Baby Bones

During my childhood, I had an experience at the beach in California that rivals the one I had on Maui last year. Were they related? I guess I'll never know.

Way back when, when I was five, my family and I took a trip to Stinson Beach, north of Maverick's where Hawaiian surfer Mark Foo died in 1995. My recollection of what happened on my childhood trip to Stinson is still as clear today as the day it happened.

I had one of those Styrofoam bodyboards you see most tourists with nowadays. I'd promised my mom I wouldn't go out in the water and that I would be "real careful." But I was intent on going out in the waves.

Once I mustered up enough courage to go out, I found myself stuck in the rip. For anyone who isn't familiar with rip currents, they suck you out to sea. That's exactly what happened to me.

I did exactly what you're not supposed to do. I panicked! I just remember looking down in the water then blacking out. Then, I remember seeing and talking to The Man we're all eventually going to meet and making a promise to him that to this day I don't know whether I've kept.

Next thing, after seeing this "light" everyone says they see in near-death experiences, I woke up on the beach with my bodyboard eighty yards away.

Fast forward to Maui. I'm twenty-nine and have been living here on Maui for six years now. I used to think "chicken skin" was something you had for dinner, but I was about to find out a new meaning.

During a big swell, I was out windsurfing at Ho'okipa and broke some equipment, as usual. So I paddled my gear down to the next reef to get out. I made it over the reef and onto the sand and started walking up to the road, where I noticed some bones.

It looked like part of a rib cage. I put down my equipment and examined it a little bit closer. It looked human. There were fragments of shell and lots of small bones and little teeth. I brushed away more sand and found the jawbone of an infant.

Along with the remains I found a piece of shell that was carved to resemble a fishhook. As soon as I discovered all of this I notified the police, but when they arrived they chuckled and said, "We know about this beach," and then drove off.

I then tried to notify the Burial Committee and also called Hawaiian Affairs. That night, I neatly placed all the bones in a towel along with the fishhook artifact and put it where it would not be disturbed.

When I went to bed, as soon as I closed my eyes, this image, like a strobe light, appeared, and in front of this light was the baby's skull.

I quickly opened my eyes, waited a long time, and closed them again. Still the same vision.

The next day, I went sailing out at Ho'okipa again, but the wind was really light and I got stranded. Guess where. You want some chicken skin? You asked for it. Right in front of where I found the baby. My hairs were standing on end.

The next day I told the Hawaiian family who watches my son what happened. They were all fascinated. I asked them if they could contact someone and tell them about the bones.

A little while after this, the granddaughter of this family was struck in the head by a stray bullet on a *heiau*. The only thing I could think to do was hold the fishhook I found in my hand and chant. I didn't even know what I was saying.

A week later the doctors were calling it a miracle. She came out of her coma and was released from Queen's on O'ahu and allowed to return home. When I saw her she gave me a big smile and I gave her one back.

Jeff Hitchcock is a professional windsurfer who also shapes surfboards and sailboards on Maui. "Baby Bones" was chosen as Third Runner-Up in the 1997 story competition.

In Hawai'i, stones on golf courses are often more than tee markers or hazards. Sometimes they work in favor of players who show respect, as champion golfer Ben Crenshaw learned in . . .

Kapu *Golf*

One night I saw Ben Crenshaw, the pro golfer, on TV telling how he had won a golfing championship in 1995 on one of the Hawaiian islands. It seems that for whatever reason the old Hawaiians had placed stones on top of one another and in a line. When the golf course was built, the stones weren't disturbed, and a line of stones ran between two holes of the course.

Crenshaw explained that for some reason he and his caddie knew they were not to cross the stones but go around them. The other golfers and caddies, who were beating him at the time, didn't know or didn't care and walked over the stones. On the next hole, Ben won the championship by hitting a shot into the hole from far off the green. An amazing shot.

Afterward, an old Hawaiian told him the spirits let him win because he showed them respect by not walking over the stones.

Allen B. Tillett, Sr., lives in Hope Mills, North Carolina, at Cypress Lakes Golf Course. Retired after thirty years in electronics with the Naval Shipyards and FAA, he enjoys golf and reading.

On Oʻahu's Windward side, just off the busy Pali Highway, almost hidden behind a YMCA, is one of Oʻahu's most sacred ancient sites—the Ulupō Heiau. Strange things occur here, especially to anyone who fails to pay proper respect, as a *malihini* learned when she suffered the consequences after her . . .

Encounter at Ulupō Heiau

Many people come to visit Ulupō Heiau. It's a place of ancient worship, but not an active place. Or so it's thought, yet strange things happen there. Sometimes our bus won't start after we visit, especially if somebody stepped on the rocks. Once, the bus doors started opening and shutting all by themselves. A girl who lives nearby told me she found baby footprints in the soft mud down by the stream. The footprints started going around in a circle, and in the circle she found dried chicken bones. The police were called, but I never heard an explanation or saw anything in the newspaper. I have heard that people who live near the *heiau* regularly see fireballs shoot across the stones at night. I don't doubt these things happen.

One Saturday night about two years ago, while I was leading a tour to the *heiau*, something very unusual happened to me.

Every Saturday night we leave by bus at sunset for Ulupō Heiau. We start at Punchbowl and go to Mānoa Cemetery, then around Sandy Beach, through Waimānalo to the *heiau*.

By the time we get to Ulupō Heiau, at about 9:15 or 9:30 p.m., it's very dark. It's really beautiful, because the *heiau* is lighted by the moon, the Kawainui Swamp is still, and the Pali is silhouetted by the glow of Honolulu's city lights. It's naturally eerie, it is.

On this particular tour we had fifty-seven people, a busload, all employees of an Oʻahu hotel on a cultural field trip to see

Oʻahu's sacred and spiritual sites. They were a great group, really excited, and they brought things to eat like *manapua*, joking that everybody has to eat it because we're going back over the Pali and you can't take pork over the Pali. It was just a real funny group.

Three older local Hawaiian ladies came up to me before the tour started and said—I thought they were joking but they were serious—that one of their colleagues, a young lady who had just recently moved from the mainland, was very skeptical about all the stories she'd heard. She was the type who would do exactly what you told her not to.

"Are you sure? Is she really going to be that bad?" I asked them, and they said, "Well, we wouldn't put anything past her."

I did notice one young woman, sitting off to the side by herself, sort of smirking, and I guessed correctly it was her.

On the way, I briefed everyone about how very important it is to show respect, that it is sacred ground. I told them not to walk on the *heiau* or remove any stones, and even if they may not believe in the Hawaiian ways, to at least pay as much respect as possible.

As everyone got off the bus we gave them a ti leaf, because it's supposed to keep you safe and bring good luck. And we used it like a ticket to get back on the bus.

After about fifteen minutes, I started walking back toward the beginning of the *heiau* and I saw those three older Hawaiian ladies, two on their knees on the ground and one standing up just shaking her head. Two of them were crying and the other was praying, chanting. I was in shock. I thought maybe it's their family's *heiau* or maybe they feel something here. Then one of the ladies pointed toward the *heiau* and said, "See, I told you. I told you."

I turned around and looked and that lady they had told me about earlier was out in the middle of the *heiau*, looking around, standing with her hands on her hips. kicking stones, saying, "What is the big deal. It's a big pile of rocks. Get over it. You're supposed to worship this thing? What's the big deal?"

My mouth just dropped open. You could hear everybody mumbling. Omigosh, you know, like "What does she think she's doing?" I didn't know how to handle this. It was so out of control at this point.

So I begged her not to desecrate the *heiau* anymore by kicking stones, and, finally, she walked back down on what's called the *menehune* pathway—it's the entrance to the *heiau*, a flat, paved trail—and came back to the group. And she had her hands on her hips still and was kind of rolling her eyes, saying, "I don't understand."

Two Hawaiian ladies opened their purses and took out some Hawaiian salt, and they started dousing her down with salt to get rid of the evil spirits. Someone had a bottle of water and they doused her with that and waved ti leaves at her.

"Oh, please just don't bother," she said. "I'm fine. There's nothing here."

All at once, several men and women started opening their wallets and purses and taking out money. They were talking about calling a cab to take her home. They believed she had caused such disrespect that spirits would follow her on the bus up over the Pali, the very dangerous part of the island, and that something would happen to her and everyone on the bus. They thought spirits would follow her and the tour would be doomed.

They doctored her with more salt and water and ti leaves and finally they agreed to get back on the bus with her, which really shocked me. The whole rest of the tour was melancholy; everybody's mood changed. You could feel the tension. We got back to the starting point, and she just sort of snuck away while the others stood shaking their heads.

Next day, when the young lady went to work, she went up to the Hawaiian ladies, lifted up her dress, and showed them her legs. They were all red and puffy and had swollen three or four times normal size. She was having difficulty walking. She was in tears.

She went to a doctor and he said, "Well, your blood is not circulating. That's why you have puffiness and swelling, but there's no physical reason this should be taking place."

She asked the three Hawaiian ladies for help, and they took her to a *kahu* and the *kahu* immediately noticed that she appeared to be dragging around extra spirits.

"What do you mean?" she asked.

"They are grabbing onto your ankles so tightly it's cutting off your circulation," he said.

So a blessing was said and she went back to Ulupō Heiau and left an offering and apologized. Her legs, of course, returned to normal size. The last we heard she was taking courses in Hawaiian Studies at University of Hawai'i-Mānoa so she wouldn't make the same mistake again.

Kim-Erin Riley is a tour guide for Hawai'i Ghost Tours, which over the last three years has taken more than four thousand residents on guided cultural tours to sacred sites on O'ahu, including the Royal Mausoleum, Mānoa Cemetery, and Ulupō Heiau.

Ulupō Heiau

Neighbors often see fireballs shoot across Windward Oʻahu's Ulupō Heiau, a massive stack of boulders imported by hand from the Waiʻanae Coast on the leeward side of the island.

With a commanding view of Kawainui Swamp and the Koʻolaus, this ancient agricultural *heiau* stands 30 feet high with a 140- by 180-foot platform. A foot path of smooth stones leads out across the *heiau* to a former grass house site.

Ulupō means "night inspiration"; the best time to visit is on a full moon night. Bring a ti leaf and Hawaiian salt in case you awaken the spirits who haunt the swamp.

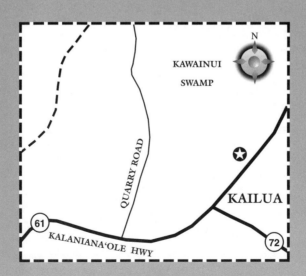

SCOTT WHITNEY

The Tree That Speaks Hawaiian

The gnarled imposing *kamani* tree has always been the first challenge to visitors to the Royal Mausoleum in Nuʻuanu. One of its huge, improbable limbs hangs directly over the iron gate entrance on Nuʻuanu Avenue, like a massive guardian wood sprite, daring the visitor to enter the sacred burial grounds of Hawaiʻi's departed monarchs.

The 3.7-acre site, on former taro lands just above Kapena Falls, was chosen by Queen Emma and King Kamehameha IV after Pohukaina, on the grounds of ʻIolani Palace, was filled up in the mid-nineteenth century. King Kamehameha V named the Nuʻuanu site Maunaʻala, or Fragrant Mountain.

According to lore, if you are quiet as you walk under this bent old tree, you might hear it speak to you, usually in old, formal chant-like Hawaiian.

It happened to Lydia Namahana Maiʻoho, the former curator of the Royal Mausoleum, who has lived on these grounds for more than thirty years.

"One night I was coming home from a function in Nānākuli," she said. "I stopped to unlock the gate. As I came inside and was closing the gate, I heard this voice above me saying, "Namahana! Namahana!"

"I was so scared," she said, "I just ran up to the house and locked the door.

"Later some Hawaiians who lived in Nuʻuanu told me they often hear the tree chanting or calling to them when they walk by Maunaʻala. The main thing, they told me, was never to answer back."

Scott Whitney is a freelance writer who is also a contributing editor to *Honolulu* magazine and *Island Business*. "The Tree That Speaks Hawaiian" first appeared as part of a longer article in *Spirit of Aloha*, June 1995.

Royal Mausoleum

In the cool highlands of Nuʻuanu, a tall iron gate protects the Royal Mausoleum, the final resting place of Hawaiʻi's kings and queens.

The Mausoleum contains the remains of King Kamehameha II, III, IV and V as well as King David Kalākaua and Queen Liliʻuokalani, the last remaining monarchs. Only one royal is missing— Kamehameha I, the last king to be buried in secret, according to old Hawaiian custom.

Only the Hawaiian flag flies over this 3.7-acre patch of sacred land dedicated in 1865 and never surrendered to America. It is the last Hawaiian place.

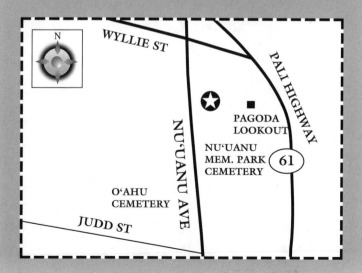

An 'aumakua stone from Kaua'i, two 'ulu maika stones from Makapu'u, old samurai swords, a silk Japanese flag with the Rising Sun over a map of the Pacific. Everything has a place. And there is a place for everything. Most of the time, things are where they are supposed to be. Sometimes, when they are moved, strange things happen. A man suffers a punishing headache, rocks roll around in the night, samurai swords bring bad luck, a silk Japanese flag from World War II gives a dying man a pang of conscience. Put back the misplaced objects and order is restored—not always, but it happens just enough to make you wonder about . . .

The Secret Life of Things

My father, the World War II pilot, was dying and he was divesting himself of small worldly possessions that once, a half century ago, meant a great deal to him, his silver wings and major's Oak Leaf, World War II medals, the Distinguished Flying Cross, Croix de Guerre, and Purple Heart; his two leather-bound war journals, one for the European Theater, the other for the Pacific, his .45-caliber pistol, and a silk Japanese flag emblazoned with the Rising Sun over a map of the Pacific. He had captured the flag as a trophy of war, and along with his medals and pistol it had reposed in a footlocker in the attic since the day he came home from the war in 1945. He never told me how he got the flag.

"Since you live in Hawai'i," he said, "maybe you can find out who the flag belongs to and return it for me."

After all these years I knew it was an impossible request, but during the fiftieth anniversary of Pearl Harbor, in Honolulu, I did meet two Japanese survivors of the war at the National Memorial Cemetery of the Pacific and showed them the flag. They examined both sides and read the katakana characters and bowed and gave it back to me. They said it would be impossible to trace the owner since no name appeared on the flag.

Later, I took the old silk flag to a Kailua antique shop, where I found the proprietor, Brad Adams, fixing an old English clock, one of dozens that surround him along with an amazing array of goods that over the years somehow surfaced on O'ahu. Stuff like a framed portrait of a cat by Beniamino Bufano, nineteenth-century bronzes like *Youth Vanquishing Serpents,* an engineer's ship model of the SS *Pearl Moore,* a whaler's harpoon gun, a moth-eaten tiger rug, a flotilla of lead models of World War II ships used to plot War Room naval maneuvers.

I showed him the Japanese silk flag with the Rising Sun over a map of the Pacific. From a shelf behind his counter he took a book big as the *Oxford English Dictionary* that showed the list price of military souvenirs from the Civil War to the Gulf War.

On a page of flags he found one that looked like the one in my hand. It was seventy-five dollars, he said. I didn't want to sell it, I told him, only trace its origin and return it. My dying father's request.

"Oh, no," Adams said. "You can't return it; it would bring great shame upon the family. They don't want it. You should keep it. Or sell it."

Since the silk flag had been in my father's footlocker since 1945, I decided to keep it as an heirloom.

Adams and I talked about the value of World War II souvenirs, and then I noticed his glass case full of old Hawai'i artifacts—adzes, chisels, and pounders—the sort of relics you see in museums. I was surprised to see so many Hawaiian artifacts in an antique shop. I guess I figured they'd all been scooped up by missionaries or salted away in the Bishop Museum.

"Does any of this old Hawaiian stuff ever give you chicken skin?" I asked. He looked me square in the eye and said matter-of-factly: "I don't believe in any of that, but a few years ago, a construction worker came in from Kaua'i with a big red 'aumakua stone about as big as a human head that looked like a turtle."

An 'aumakua is a family spirit guardian, an owl, a turtle, or a shark, and when a stone is found with animal characteristics, it is believed by Hawaiians to have special powers.

"When Hurricane 'Iniki swept Kaua'i, it knocked down a lot of shacks on the coast and rearranged the landscape, and that *'aumakua* came out of the ground with some poi pounders and a lot of other stuff.

"The construction worker brought the *'aumakua* back to Honolulu and put it outside his house. His wife didn't want it in the house. She didn't like it. His wife said, 'Get rid of it.' He came in one day and wanted to sell it. I gave him $100.

"Right after he sold it to me, he broke his back in a construction accident. He was hung up for a couple of years.

"That stone, it was something else," he said. "Every time it was near me, I got beating headaches. And after we got that stone, the shop didn't make any money.

"I didn't pay any attention to the rock until my wife, who's Hawaiian, said, 'You've got headaches because you bought an *'aumakua*. It's got to be put up above your head.'

"When I finally put it up on the shelf over my head, my headaches went away and business picked up. If I had it in front of me or facing me, I'd get a headache again.

"After about a year, I told my wife, 'Let's get rid of it.' I just gave it away. It wasn't for us to have. She put it in a friend's garden. Now, all the plants around it are growing like hell. Oh yeah!

"The new people with the stone took it to some old Hawaiian lady, and she said it was an alien."

"Meaning what?" I asked. "Something not from Hawai'i? Or not from Earth?"

"I don't know," he said. "She just said that this stone is an alien stone. That's all she said."

"How did the stone cause your headaches?" I asked.

"Who knows," he said. "You tell me. I'll tell you what though, I'm not superstitious. I don't believe in all that spirit stuff. I'm a Christian, and Christians don't believe in that.

"You know," he said, "there is so much stuff in this world that people collect and get rid of, and it ends up in shops like mine, and the trouble it may have caused them doesn't transfer.

"We've had other 'aumakua stones in here and never had a problem," he said. "Nothing ever happened to me before that 'aumakua stone.

"It's all just superstition," he said. "Like my mother is Japanese, and she will tell you that you cannot own a Japanese sword. It's bad luck, bad things will happen to you.

"I collect plenty of old Japanese swords and no harm has come to me, but I know a guy in his seventies who collected swords his whole life and about twenty-five years ago he just had a run of bad luck and a Japanese priest said get rid of his swords and he did and everything cleared right up. Coincidence, right?

"This other guy I know, an old Japanese man, he was telling me this story. He went looking for moss rocks at Makapu'u Point and he found two round stones. I think they were used for Hawaiian bowling. He took the stones home, put them in his house in Kailua, in his living room. He went to bed and that night the whole house was shaking.

"He got up the next morning. The two stones were touching each other. He separated them. The next morning, the two stones were three feet apart. He took the stones back to Makapu'u and left them over there.

"Who can explain it? I think it's imagination. Imagination gets a hold of you and people get carried away."

"Did you imagine your headaches?" I asked.

"I have no idea," he said. "Could be my imagination. Yeah, that's probably what it was. Who knows?

"All I know is I bought that rock on a Saturday afternoon about one o'clock and it sat right here on my glass case about two feet away from me and right away I had a headache. It was really bad. I just wanted it out of the shop."

The new keepers of the *'aumakua* stone, Adams said, have experienced no problems.

Maybe some things are just meant to be in certain places, I told him. He just shrugged. Neither one of us knew the answer.

My father died a few months later, and his ashes were scattered at sea. His memorial service was conducted with military honors. When the honor guards slowly folded the American flag into a tight triangle and handed it to my mother, I thought of my father's life as a warrior and remembered his Japanese silk flag with the Rising Sun over a map of the Pacific.

The silk flag reposes now at my house in a Japanese tansu with my father's silver wings and hero medals. When I see the silk flag, I think of my father and always wonder how it fell into his hands and if somewhere in Tokyo today there is an old Japanese woman who lost her husband in the war, an old Japanese woman without a flag. I wonder, too, if it matters to her or anyone but me now.

Rick Carroll is now at work on *Travelers' Tales Hawaii* (O'Reilly & Associates, San Francisco), an anthology of personal discoveries in the Hawaiian Islands.

When Keala Binz was eleven years old, her father encountered an odd-shaped stone on a construction project that caused strange things to happen at night in Waialua.

The Stone

It had been a normal day—get up early, go to school, come home, do homework, eat dinner, and then go to bed. But that night was totally different.

I should tell you I was about eleven years old. It was 1989. I attended Kamehameha Schools then, and I usually caught a ride with my uncle and my cousin into Wahiawā to the bus stop. You see, I'm from Waialua on the north shore of O'ahu. As I was saying, that night was extremely strange.

I am a very heavy sleeper, but for some strange reason I woke up at four in the morning. I was wide awake and I did not know why. Only seconds after I awoke did I hear a car pull up outside. I even saw lights flash against my walls. I heard the engine turn off, footsteps outside on the porch, and then a knocking on the front door.

"Keala, wake up Keala, I'm here to take you to school," the voice said.

I could've sworn it was my uncle, but it was four o' clock in the morning.

Well, I was taught never to answer anyone who calls for you at night, but in my curiosity I opened my window to peer outside. In front of my window was a ghost. All I could see was the silhouette. The ghost was transparent, but at the same time looked very solid, almost like a cloud.

Chicken skin overtook my body. Chills ran up and down my

spine. I knew it could not hurt me, but still I was afraid, so afraid I could hardly breathe. I ran to my mom and dad's room and told them what happened.

I found out later that the ghost followed my dad home from work. My dad was a construction worker, and the day this occurred one of his co-workers had brought a stone in the shape of a chair to work.

Now, my dad is pure *haole*, but he was raised by his *hānai* family to respect the ways of old Hawai'i. He told his co-worker, "Put that stone back where you found it. You should never remove a stone from its place of rest."

Because the man had moved the stone and then took it to the place where my dad worked, the ghost followed my dad home from work and came to make trouble for his family.

The day after I saw the ghost, my dad went back to work and found the co-worker who had the stone. He backed him into a corner and asked him, "Did you take the stone back like I told you?"

"No, I don't believe in that stuff," the guy said.

Well, that did it. My dad told his co-worker the whole story. And he took the stone back to its original location and left it there for good.

This time when my dad came home, no troubled spirits followed.

And that was the end of my sleep being bothered by the ghost.

Eighteen-year-old Keala Binz has lived all her life in Waialua, O'ahu. This story is one of the many spooky things that have happened to her or to someone in her family.

Kāhuna

....

N obody believed Tim's mother was a *kahuna* with supernatural powers until the screaming started one Sunday afternoon at Peyton Place Far West. Then everybody knew . . .

Mama Was a Kahuna

It was in the late '60's. We were single and (somewhat) care-free. Jill and I lived in a self-made singles apartment on the slopes of Punchbowl. The Vietnam war was still going strong—and sending the military to Hawai'i for R & R.

For one military man, Tim, R & R was good. Hawai'i was home. For Tim, it was Mom's *haupia*, sun and surf, and his girl, Maria. Tim's mother, being full-blooded Hawaiian, was hoping for a Hawaiian daughter-in-law. But, alas, Maria was a *haole* from Brooklyn.

Mama did not easily accept Maria, and each time Tim came home on leave, Maria would become almost deathly ill, with no explanation for the illness. Maria, who was a nurse, insisted Mama had *kahuna* powers and was sending spirits to harm her.

We all laughed and told her she was imagining things. But on one lazy Sunday afternoon we became believers.

Music floated around the building. A couple of guys washed their cars. All was pretty quiet at the high-rise next door.

I first heard some screams from down the hall, but figured it was the makings of an afternoon party. (Better check the beer and pupu supplies.) Then, in a flash, there were pounding footsteps as our neighbor, Barb, Maria's roommate, went racing past our front door. Party time, I thought. She'll be in the pool shortly, like it or not.

I sat there waiting for the other shoe to drop—the chaser. But nobody else went by. Some time passed, and I figured the party had fizzled. Oh, well, back to the Sunday paper and my beer. Just 'cause there's no party, no sense wasting a Primo!

Then the screaming started again. A door slammed shut. Pounding, running footsteps again. Before I could get to the door to investigate, Barb stood in our living room looking whiter than her natural *haole* tones. Out of breath and stuttering, she spit out, "It's haunted! I can't stay there!"

Jill came out to check on the commotion and as we calmed Barb down, the story emerged. Tim was home on leave and came over to take Maria out. Barb was reading the paper when an eerie presence took over the living room. A strange, burning odor, a haze, and the feeling of someone else in the room. Barb checked the bathroom, the two bedrooms, the lanai, and the pool area on the other side of her lanai wall. Nothing. Except back in the living room, whatever it was was still there.

We calmed Barb down and went back to her apartment to play super sleuth and investigate. Upon entering the apartment we were greeted with an eerie odor—and it wasn't incense!

Barb, Maria, Jill and I all believed in Hawaiian folklore, and never took pork over the Pali. Jill and I even had a tiki facing the front door just to be safe. So Jill went back to our apartment to get Barb some supplies. When she returned she had a dozen or so ti leaves, our tiki, and Hawaiian salt. She put the tiki facing the front door. Then, room by room, she placed ti leaves and salt on tables and counters.

The unknown presence dissolved. Barb regained some of her color. Jill and I went home. We discussed the matter and concluded that it was Tim's mother. For whatever reason, her powers were being distracted and she was spooking the wrong *haole*.

The rest of the day went by quietly. Jill and I retired for

the night. As I closed my door and turned out my light, I noticed a light come on in the hallway and shine under my door. I figured Jill forgot something, although I never heard any movement.

The next evening I casually mentioned to Jill that I had seen the light go on and asked her what she forgot. Jill said "Me? I thought you went back out and wondered if you were okay, but I didn't hear anything and then the light went out, so I went to sleep."

We stared at each other for all of five seconds before we bolted for the door. It was a footrace, three apartment lengths, to Barb and Maria's. We raced in and made a dive for the tiki. With both of us clutching the tiki, we told Barb and Maria to keep the salt and ti leaves. We needed the tiki. Mama visited us last night!

After that incident, things at Peyton Place Far West (as we nicknamed our singles complex) settled down to the usual routine—work, party, work, party, party.

The incident was never explained, but it did leave four young *haole* ladies truly believing in the Hawaiian supernatural.

Linda Liddell has worked as a clown, a manicurist, a respiratory technician, a small-town newspaper columnist, and a travel agent. Born in Rochester, New York, she grew up in San Diego, California, and now lives on Moloka'i, her favorite place of all. "Mama Was a *Kahuna*" was awarded an Honorable Mention in the 1997 story competition.

Be careful not to step on
any sacred rocks if you go
hunting in Hawai‘i or
you may end up like the
hapless victim in
Darlynn D. Donohue's
eerie story . . .

Hunting on Lāna'i

About ten years ago, my father went hunting with some friends on Lāna'i. At some point he became deathly ill and they sent him back to Honolulu. He was in the hospital for about a week. During that time, they brought in many doctors because no one could figure out what was wrong with him. If he stood up and tried to walk to a point in the room, he would end up on the complete opposite end of the room. The only way he could navigate was by holding onto my brother's shoulder.

I kept calling home (I was living on the mainland) to ask if I needed to make a trip back to see my dad. On the sixth day, I called my mom and said I was coming. She said to wait because my sister had called a *kahuna* and they were going to try something.

I have always been skeptical about kahunas and all the other crazy stuff that goes on in Hawai'i, but I have seen enough to know that when my family says do something, I do it. Once, I ran over a dog and my mom made me sprinkle Hawaiian salt in the car. I told her she was crazy, but I sprinkled the salt. She always reminds me when I go to the Big Island not to take anything out of the volcano. I laugh when she says this, but I give other people going to Hawai'i the same advice. So I said my sister was crazy for calling the *kahuna*, but . . .

The next morning, I got a call saying that my dad would be fine and I didn't need to fly home. The *kahuna* said he apparently stepped in a *heiau* when he was hunting and that's what caused his illness. The *kahuna* took my father's clothes away and did something to them. Is it a coincidence that he got well the next day? To this day, we have no explanation for his illness (and neither do the doctors).

When I ask my father about the incident, he just shrugs his shoulders and says, "Who knows what happened?" I think he's also a skeptic, but it's hard to remain skeptical when something like this happens.

Darlynn D. Donohue grew up in Hawai'i and joined the Air Force when she was seventeen. After leaving the service, she lived in Colorado for sixteen years. She now lives in Phoenix, Arizona, where she is a Senior Consultant for Oracle Corporation.

Haleakalā Crater

Some say Haleakalā Crater is a "power spot," a natural conductor of cosmic energy. Others claim it "accelerates personal growth." I don't know about any of that, but Hawaiian *kāhuna* did use the Earth's biggest dormant volcano as a temple to conduct sacred rites. There are stories of epic battles between healers and sorcerers; old bones are still found in caves.

In modern days, NASA's astronauts trained in the lunar-like crater for the Apollo moonshot. On the rim of the crater are seven mysterious silver domes where scientists observe the sun, bounce lasers off the moon and monitor space traffic.

In one dome, known as the Maui Space Surveillance Site, the U.S. Air Force uses a 3.7-meter Advance Electro-Optical System Telescope in the constant search for alien spacecraft.

More than 1.3 million folks go up to the 10,023-foot-high mountain for sunrise, but few stick around for sundown. Even fewer venture deeper into the crater. To be all alone inside the crater after dark is to feel like the last human on Earth.

An odd-shaped artifact
found in a cave on the
Kona Coast of the
Big Island of Hawai'i
takes on a life of its own
in this classic story.

The Poi Pounder

I have a friend who has a great love for things Hawaiian. All his life he has known Hawaiians and feels their mystique with great sympathy. And all his life he has collected Hawaiiana—stone adzes, bowls, ancient implements like bone fishhooks and carrying gourds, akuas, the curiously shaped gods of households, stone poi pounders, coral files and needles and many other fascinating objects. His house is a small museum.

We camped once together in a place called Kapu'a, deep down on the Kona Coast, far away from the world, and walked for miles round the deserted old *heiau*, the flat stone temples of long ago, the village sites, the grave mounds and the thin ribbons of smooth stone trails. There is an old *hōlua* there, a sled slide looking like a piece of cinder highway placed on a hillside. In past days the Hawaiians made sleds, covered the slope with ti leaves and raced down the incline on the green slickness. Standing there, it was not hard to imagine the gala in the sun, the shouts and laughs and cheers, the color of feathered capes and gleaming brown bodies. Now it is a stillness place, only the sea moves and sparkles.

We found a small cave, hidden under a *kiawe* thicket under the sharp drop of the *hōlua*. We squatted on its cinder floor, enjoying its shade. Then we started scraping in the earth among the seashells and twigs, looking for bone fishhooks or *'ulu maika*, the smooth-shaped small stone discs the Hawaiians used for their bowling games. Finding nothing, my friend started examining the walls. Suddenly, he said, as if knowing, "I think it's up here."

He reached over my head and pulled dry dirt and stones from a tiny recess. Magically, he brought forth a long poi-pounder–shaped piece of stone, about nine inches long and perfectly formed. "This is a good one," he said, "a very unusual shape."

We walked back along the beach to our camp, for dusk was falling. We passed a rotting canoe, forlorn in the long rays of the sun, half-hidden in the tall grass.

Back in camp, we built a fire for supper and my friend washed the stone clean. He said he had a curious feeling about his find. It was not an ordinary pounder, he said. More likely it was a *kahuna* pestle, used by the priests for grinding medicine or potions. "I have an odd feeling about this stone," he said. "I think it has *mana*. I can feel its *mana*." Before we slept he carefully placed the stone on a box near our bedrolls.

In the morning it had disappeared. We scoured the area, looking everywhere, but it was gone. And we were the only humans for many miles.

Ed Sheehan came to Hawai'i in 1940 as a sheet metal worker at Pearl Harbor Naval Shipyard. He survived the December 7, 1941, Japanese air raid and stayed on in the Islands as a jack-of-all-trades, working as an itinerant fisherman, a stonecarver, a radio announcer and a Honolulu newspaper columnist before emerging as Hawai'i's premier storyteller. Among his many works are *Days of '41*, recalling events of that fateful year, and *The Hawaiians*, from which this story is excerpted.

Haunted Places

....

Lights go on and off.
A pen floats in mid-air.
A Honolulu property manager
encounters the supernatural
when he goes alone
in broad daylight
to inspect . . .

The Vacant Apartment

In December of 1993, our firm took over the property management of an apartment complex with some commercial tenants on the ground floor.

This three-story building has a total of twenty-two residential studios. At the time, only one studio on the back end of the building on the third floor was occupied—by only one tenant. My job initially was to inspect the twenty-one vacant units located on the second and third floors (eleven units to a floor).

The inspection of each unit was done to find what discrepancies were there at present, what needed correction, so that a budget could be made to determine approximate costs for repairs and follow-ups. When we took over the account, the representatives of the owners told us some work had been done, but left incomplete, by their handymen.

I was alone to do the inspection. I had with me my leather folder, pens, and inspection report forms.

I began my inspection with Unit 201. As I went into the unit, which was quite small, I went straight ahead into the bathroom and turned on the lights so that I could see what I was writing.

Inside the bathroom were three lights (two on either side of the bath basin and one above the shower stall). While I was opening the shower door, the light directly above the shower stall suddenly clicked off. This gave me a slight chill. I turned my head to the light switch and found that the light switch was still in the

ON position and the other lights were still working. Naturally, I thought the light bulb had just died. I finished up writing the inspection comments for the bathroom and proceeded to inspect the living area.

Within thirty seconds of coming out of the bathroom, while I was standing facing the bathroom entry writing comments on the inspection report on my notepad, something caught my eye and made me look up. About three feet away from me, at the top of the ceiling, I saw one of my writing pens suspended vertically by itself for more than a brief moment. When I turned my head to look at it directly, it then fell straight down to the floor.

Yikes! the hairs on the back of my neck rose and I wanted to run out.

However, I picked up that pen (which was one of three pens that were in my aloha shirt pocket), quickly walked out and locked the door and walked down to talk to ANYBODY. The hairs on my neck were still raised, as nothing like this has ever happened to me in my life.

I spoke to the manager of a nearby tourist convenience store at that time, and he said that he knew nothing about any ghosts in any of the units, only that one person had died in another unit upstairs.

I told him I would never go back into that unit by myself. However, I had to inspect the remaining twenty vacant units that day and nothing else happened.

I told the story to many people at work, and some of them told me that the area used to be a burial ground for Hawaiians. I really don't know what to say or how to explain this supernatural occurrence but it did happen. Since that time, there have not been any supernatural occurrences, as far as we know. We even have a tenant living in Unit 201.

Dennis Yanos lives in Honolulu with his wife, Jodie, and son, Alden. A graduate of the University of Hawai'i, he has worked since 1987 for the property management firm that manages the building where this inexplicable occurrence took place. "The Vacant Apartment" was awarded an Honorable Mention in the 1997 story competition.

Odd noises, a tall shadow,
strange footsteps, a face in
the second story window,
conversations from an
empty room.
Despite repeated
blessings by a *kahuna*,
weird occurrences keep
happening in . . .

Jason's House

This happened about five years ago. I was living in the dorms at UH. My father went on a business trip, and I moved in to watch the house. My parents are divorced, so I had the house to myself.

Really weird things started happening. I would be at home, studying for finals coming up, and would get the feeling of someone else present in the room. I would see something, almost always in the silhouette of a large male, six foot six, maybe seven feet—very tall. It would usually be in a certain doorway, filling the doorframe. I'd sense it and try to ignore it. It would get stronger, and eventually I'd look up, only to see it, then watch it disappear at almost the same moment. I remember sitting at the table studying, and although I was looking at my work on the table, with my peripheral vision I would be able to see snakelike objects slithering across the floor.

I finally told a friend at work, Tim, about the weird occurrences around my house. I deliberately left things vague. I told him I was seeing things that weren't really there, but no specifics. He was from Indiana, and had at one time been involved in a satanic cult. He managed to get out, and had a passing interest in spooky stuff. He offered to come over and spend the night. If anything happened, he'd be there. He didn't drive, so I picked him up, then left him at my house and went to pick up a girl I was seeing at the time and bring her over.

Larni, Tim, and I settled into the living room to watch TV. Within ten minutes, I was asleep, and slept through the night. I woke up the next morning to find Tim asleep under a table, and Larni on the sofa. Both awoke shortly after me. Tim looked terrible. It was obvious he hadn't slept well. They told me that after I fell asleep, Larni saw something. She described the same six-foot-six or seven-foot shadow I had been seeing, and also described it as filling the doorframe. I was scared, because I hadn't told them about any of this. Tim didn't see anything. He did, however, spend the night under the table dry-heaving, with stomach cramps. He said that when he was trying to get out of the cult he was in, he would go to sleep, only to wake in the middle of the night with dry heaves and stomach cramps, exactly as he had the previous night. He said he had the experience nightly until he success-fully got out, and hadn't had the same experience since.

After that, I left the house and went to my dorm until my dad returned. I told him all about it, and he arranged to have the house blessed by a *kahuna*. The weird things stopped. I guess that would be the end of the story, but because of that experience, I started talking to my dad and mom about other weird occurrences at the house. Both of them, who haven't talked at length to each other in almost fifteen years, told me the same stories.

A couple months after I was born, my mom put me down for a nap. I was only a couple of months old, and could barely move, let alone crawl. My mom says the blanket was in the corner of the crib, out of my reach, and definitely not on me. She heard "strange noises" coming from the room and came in to find the blanket wrapped around my neck.

She also said that when she hung the clothes to dry, and later picked them off the line and folded them into neat piles, she would later find all the clothes in a big messed-up pile on the floor. In addition, she said she would be home alone, but hear conversations in other rooms, only to find them empty. She would also hear footsteps across the house when she was the only one home. I can attest to this, as I, and close friends who come over, too, have heard mysterious conversations and footsteps. A friend of mine once claimed to have seen a face in the window looking in, except that the window is over seven feet off the ground.

My parents had a *kahuna* bless the house more than once, and also made offerings of *laulau*, *kālua* pig, and other Hawaiian foods for a period of seven days. After that, the occurrences stopped for a while, but then eventually happened again.

After the incident five years ago, all of the previous occurrences came to light, and it seems they were following a pattern. The events occurred every ten years—a few months after I was born, after my tenth birthday, and after my twentieth birthday. It was suggested that I have a decade ghost, or maybe even a demon coming after me at set intervals. I can't type this story without getting chicken skin.

Jason Wong has graduated from the University of Hawai'i at Mānoa and continues to experience the paranormal. He is anxiously awaiting a call from the creators of *The X-Files*.

In 1990, two small, dark, shadowy forms appear in a woman's North Shore bedroom at night. They stand at the foot of her bed. When a third figure appears, Cynthia Broc decides to solve the mystery of the . . .

North Shore Spirits

Shortly after the birth of my second son in 1990, I had a strange encounter in my home on the North Shore. Two dark, shadowy forms appeared in my bedroom at night. They would often stand at the foot of my bed, not always on the same side. After a while three forms would appear. They weren't very big forms—no taller than five feet, two of them much shorter.

At first I thought this was my imagination or sleep deprivation due to the new baby in the house. But they kept appearing. I also began to hear laughter in the house late at night and balls being bounced in the living room. Each time I got up there was no one awake in my house and the neighbors' lights were all off.

After a year of these appearances, I told my mother-in-law what I had seen. She lived next door and was very interested to find out what these sightings might be. I felt there was a great deal of sadness and fear associated with these forms.

I was never afraid for myself or my family. The forms never spoke or floated above my bed. But I was concerned that I was the only one who could see them. I didn't understand why they had come to me.

My mother-in-law relayed this story to a friend of hers who knew some history about my house. I found out through this friend that two children had been killed in my house a long time before I arrived. They had suffered a horrible death at the hands of a sibling.

When our house had to be demolished in 1994 (irreparable termite damage), I thought of a way I could help these children. I called a priest, a family friend, to come to our house prior to the demolition. The priest told me that it is believed that those who suffer horrible deaths can't find their way to put their souls to rest; they don't know whether to go to the dark or the light. So their souls stay on Earth unable to rest. I asked him to bless the house and put the children to rest.

We had a short ceremony for these children inside the house. After the holy water was sprinkled throughout the house and we said our prayers, everyone present felt a strong gust of wind blow through the house. The priest even commented afterward about the presence he felt in the house.

Awhile after the demolition and the blessing, I took a trip to California with my children. A Hawaiian healer sat next to my oldest son on the plane. We spoke about many different things during our five-hour flight. He told me he had recently started to help people on the island who were having trouble with spirits on their properties. I told him the story of the spirits in my house. I only spoke to him about the two children, because at the time I was not concerned about the third spirit I had seen.

He sat with interest as I told my story. After I was finished he looked at me and said, "You forget to tell me about the third spirit you have seen."

He told me he could see the spirit in his mind, but the place the spirit stood most often was not at the foot of my bed but at the foot of my children's bed.

It was at that moment that I knew my husband's Hawaiian uncle had indeed come back to watch over our children as he told my husband he would prior to his death in the early 1980s. My children and I have never met him, but I continue to feel his presence and know my children are blessed by it.

We are still living on the same property in a new house. I have not seen or heard the two spirits of the deceased children since our old house was demolished I hope their souls have found peace.

Originally from Connecticut, Cynthia Broc moved to Hawai'i from California in 1987. She lives on the North Shore of O'ahu with her husband, Jim, and her children, Joseph and John. She is a sales representative for Nurse Wear, which manufactures apparel in colors and patterns designed to spread aloha through the island health community. A substitute special education teacher in Windward O'ahu, she is on the advisory board of a Goodwill project called Partnership in Community. "North Shore Spirits" was awarded an Honorable Mention in the 1997 story competition.

Hurrying across the grounds of 'Iolani Palace at high noon, a Honolulu woman experiences an inexplicable incident with . . .

The Maile Lei

My first job in Honolulu was as a lei maker at the airport. When I started work there, I was told *maile* should never be entwined with anything else.

Some years later I worked at Queen's Medical Center. Just before lunch hour I was told a co-worker was having a birthday. I ran downtown to buy a lei for the occasion. The lei maker entwined *maile* and *'ilima* leis that I had selected.

I noticed the clock and was worried about getting back to work in time. So I grabbed the leis and decided to take a short-cut through 'Iolani Palace.

A few steps onto the 'Iolani Palace grounds I felt a cold, forceful hand on my right shoulder. When I turned around fast, I got chicken skin and dropped the lei.

Then I realized no one was even near enough to grab me. But when I reached down to pick up the leis, the two leis were separated in the plastic lei bag that had been sealed with a tie and ribbon at the lei stand.

Ever since that incident, I have observed deep respect when at 'Iolani Palace and have practiced good lei etiquette.

A native New Yorker and world traveler, Nancy K. Davis moved to Hawai'i on Admission Day 1967. In Hawai'i she has worked at both Queen's Medical Center and GTE Hawaiian Tel. "The *Maile* Lei" was chosen as Second Runner-Up in the 1997 story competition.

Pohukaina Mound

No kings or queens have been buried in this grave for years, but the former royal plot in downtown Honolulu between the State Capitol and City Hall remains *kapu*. That's off-limits. It's ringed by an iron fence with *kapu* signs and planted with ti to ward off evil spirits.

"The Pohukaina Mound at 'Iolani Palace perhaps sets a precedent," says archaeologist Paul Christiaan Klieger. "It is not known for certain if any human remains exist at the site of the old Honolulu Royal Museum, but due to the *mana* of prior association, at least, the spot is considered worthy of respect."

I once spent hours photographing Pohukaina Mound in different light from various angles, and none of my photographs came out.

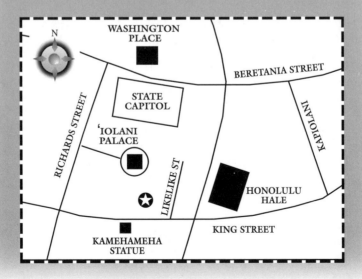

Night Terrors

If you've ever dreamed
of sleeping under a palm tree
on the golden sand of some
secluded beach in Hawai'i,
you should be prepared
to experience the extraordinary,
as Sandy Martino warns in . . .

A Night on the Beach

I was a student at Maui Community College. I had just arrived on Maui, and I decided I wanted to spend the night on the beach. The island was still quite unique to me, and I thought, "Ah, this'll be really exciting!"

I packed my big old rolling suitcase with books, food, and bedding, and had a friend drop me off at a place out past Mākena Beach, in the lava fields. I went snorkeling for a couple of hours, then came back and unpacked my stuff and lay out on the beach. I had a couple of beers and was just tuning out, listening to music on my Walkman and relaxing. Everything felt so good, so calm, that I soon fell asleep.

When I woke up, it was full dark, really dark. I wasn't where I had been when I fell asleep, and I didn't know where I was. I had been moved! I had my suitcase with me. It was all packed up, and I was out in the lava fields, quite a ways from where I had fallen asleep on the beach. I was confused and disoriented. I thought, "WHAT is going on?" The suitcase was large and weighed about a hundred pounds. I didn't pack it up and hike it up there in my sleep.

I picked the suitcase up and slung it over my back and hiked back out to the same beach where I had been originally. I had to struggle to get it back there by myself, and I'm a hefty guy. All I had on my feet was a pair of slippers, and they were totally eaten up by the sharp lava rocks on my way back. I put the suitcase down and lay back down again and fell asleep. The next thing I knew, I woke up back in the lava fields with my suitcase again! And this time, I was really, really freaked out. It is hard for me to describe how I felt.

Well, I picked my suitcase up and hiked back to the same beach—again. How I found my way back to the same beach twice in the dark, I don't know. I sat down on the beach again and it started to rain. I could feel some sort of presence around me. I was overwhelmed by it. I got up and started swearing and yelling and just flipping right out.

I sat down again and stayed on this beach all night, in the rain. In the morning it was sunny. Two people showed up, a man and a woman. I told them the story of this incredible night I'd had, and they just smiled and looked at each other and nodded their heads like they knew exactly what I was talking about.

I went and did some snorkeling and sat out there all day, waiting for the friend who had given me a ride out there to come and pick me up in the afternoon. When it got to be late in the afternoon and she hadn't shown up, I started getting anxious. Where was she? Had she forgotten about me? I knew ONE thing; I wasn't spending one more minute in the dark on that beach. So I packed up my suitcase again with all my snorkel gear and what not, lugged it up to the road, and started walking. I was a fair ways down the road away from the beach by the time my friend came along, well after dark. I got in the car and told her, "I just spent the wildest, freakiest night of my life!" and started relating some of what had happened to me.

When we got back to the MCC dorms, I went to talk to a Hawaiian fellow from Hāna. I knew he would be able to explain what had happened to me. I found him with another local guy, and I told my story to the two of them, hoping for an explanation. They smiled knowingly, and just said, "Night marchers." Apparently, the area is known for the night marchers, and I had gone to the beach on a night when they were known to pass through there.

The two men asked me if, when I went back to the beach the second time and felt the presence, I had sworn out loud. I told them, "Yeah, you're damned right! I yelled and swore my head off!" They said that may be what had saved me. I don't know. All I know is that it was a crazy experience. Before that happened, I laughed at all the supernatural stories I had heard since I got to Hawai'i. I tell you, I never laughed after that night on the beach. It was something I'll never forget. It seems unbelievable, now, but I know it happened.

Sandy Martino is a former magazine editor and writer and lifelong ghost story collector. Born and raised in the islands, she is currently an instructor at Maui Community College. This story was related to her by one of her former students, who wishes to remain anonymous. "A Night on the Beach" was chosen as First Runner-Up in the 1997 story competition.

On a dark night on the Konawaena School campus, built on an old Hawaiian cemetery, the sounds of a basketball game in progress in the gym awaken the Physical Education teacher and five others, who with flashlights in hand go to investigate . . .

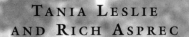
Night Games

Konawaena, which means "Center of Kona," is the name of the school I attended from kindergarten through my senior year. Like many others', my days were filled with happiness. Hanging out and talking story were part of my daily routine. That is why I was surprised to learn that Konawaena has had a rich history of ghostly, unexplained phenomena.

Many believe that strange things happen there because the upper part of the campus is built partially over the sacred trails of the night marchers. The lower part, where the old gymnasium and the current football field stand, is built upon an old Hawaiian cemetery. These are possible explanations of what may have unsettled the sleeping spirits who gave us all chicken skin.

Our school, which was the only high school on the Kona side of the Big Island until recently, is located on the slopes of Mauna Kea. The *makai* (ocean) side of the slope is where the teachers' cottages were. Because of the remote location of the school, many of the teachers lived in these bungalows during the '50s. Just *mauka* (mountain side) of the cottages was the "old" gymnasium, which burned down in 1974 for unexplained reasons.

It was an old wooden building where the local basketball games and indoor sports activities took place. Many of the teachers who lived in the bungalows were teaching there when I was enrolled, and from them I heard many stories of unexplained events.

On one particular night, the teachers, including the Physical Education teacher, were engaged in their nightly routines—reading, grading, or just preparing for bed.

Suddenly, six of them heard familiar sounds coming from the *mauka* side. They gathered on their porches and looked up to where the noises were coming from. They could hear the roar of the cheering crowd and saw the lights through the roof vents. Sure enough, it was the gym.

They asked the P.E. teacher what game was being played at this late hour. He said he had no idea. Nothing was scheduled and definitely not at this time of night. They decided to go see for themselves.

The annoyed group began to walk up the hill to investigate and end the unseemly event that had disrupted the silence of the night.

As they drew closer, they could hear the sounds of a basketball game: the echo of the backboard as a ball bounced off it, the blaring buzzers, the referees' whistles, and the dribble of the ball. Confused and curious, the teachers approached the main entrance to the gymnasium. The sounds were deafening.

They looked through the small glass windows set in the heavy wooden doors and saw only blackness; yet when they looked above, they could see light seeping out through the roof vents. How could this be, they asked themselves, as fear set in.

The P.E. teacher, feeling that his territory had been violated, cautiously pulled at the door, only to find that it was locked. He reached into his pocket and produced the key ring. Nervously, he fumbled with the lock until it opened.

He quickly tugged the door open, and simultaneously the lights from the vents became as black as the room inside. The deafening roar, heard earlier, ceased. The only sound they heard was the final echoing bounces of a ball recently dropped.

The group stood there, frightened. One of them reached for the light switch and flicked it on, only to find nothing there, not even a lonely basketball taking its final bounce.

Tania Leslie moved to California in 1987 after graduating in 1986 from Konawaena High School. She now works as a store manager in Culver City.

Rich Asprec is a struggling musician and film student at California State University Long Beach.

On a rare, rainy night on Maui, in the upcountry plantation settlement of Ha'ikū, two young women are spooked by the ghostly sight of . . .

Fading Figures

One night in the summer of '93, my friend Heather and I had absolutely nothing to do and were very bored. We decided to visit our friends in Haʻikū. We found ourselves a ride and spent a few hours laughing, joking, and just kicking back with our friends.

The night seemed to go by very fast. It started to drizzle, and there was a slight chill in the breeze. Most of us were getting cold. Since my friends live near each other, to get home they just had to walk around the block or down the road.

One by one, everyone left. Then it was only me and Heather again. We didn't want to spend the night at anyone's house. We were hungry and tired and just wanted to go home. Not wanting to bother anyone to use their phone, we decided to use the pay phone next to the cannery. It wasn't much of a journey anyway, just a ten-minute walk at the most.

We walked through the dead silent night side by side. It was still drizzling, and by then, the cold air was really getting to us. Finally, we reached the pay phone. I handed Heather a quarter from my pocket, and she proceeded to phone her mom.

As I waited, I noticed two people about fifty feet away from us, in the middle of the road. They had their backs turned to us, so I couldn't see any faces.

I tapped Heather on the arm and pointed to the road, and she saw them too. It didn't seem like they were moving, or even walking. They were very still.

Heather turned to me with a very odd expression. I was looking at her the same way.

"There wasn't anybody there before?" I asked her.

"No way," Heather said. "Nobody. Where did they come from?"

"I don't know," I said. "After I handed you the quarter, they just appeared on the road."

We were already scared. We continued to watch the figures. While we watched, they faded away into the night. There was no sign of them at all.

"Did you see that?" I asked Heather. "They just disappeared. They faded or something. What *was* that?"

"I don't know," Heather said, shaking her head. " but I saw the same thing."

Grabbing her arm, I said, "There's no way I'm waiting here."

Arm in arm, we ran back to the house and waited there for her mom, who found us scared and puzzled by what we saw. We still have no explanation.

Nicole Sarsona, who loves scary stories, lives with her parents in upcountry Maui.

Small-Kid Time

....

Muʻumuʻu

Woman in White

The Sandalwood Warrior

Hickam Ghosts

Laupāhoehoe Beach Park

The Hawaiian word *mu'umu'u* means "cut off, shortened, amputated." It's also the nickname of a scary character who haunted the "small-kid" days of Maui youngsters, as George Y. Fujita tells us in his nostalgic, prize-winning story.

Muʻumuʻu

Sometimes things happen and the events are etched so clearly in your mind that you will never forget the day. The Saturday I met Muʻumuʻu face to face would turn out that way for me.

"Yoshchan, come. I want you to buy mama some Lahaina *nasubi* today. I was going to ask Tetchan but she had to go to the library. You know what Lahaina *nasubi* is?"

"Yeah. That's the small-kine eggplant, right?"

"That's right. It's season time now. It's hard to get, so there's goin' to be plenty of people trying to buy. They'll be bringing them in on the Lahaina bus—the red and white one and it comes at eight. Okay?"

"I know, mom." My mom made the best *tsukemono* in town. Her pickles were better than my grandma's, and the purple *nasubi* ones were her specialty. Everyone knew that.

"I want you to wait for the bus, and as soon as they unload the vegetables I want you to get in line and buy me a dozen. Don't lose this money now. Can I trust you? . . ."

Market Street on Saturday is the smell of roasted peanuts, steamed pork in the *lau lau*, ginger leis, and ripe papayas. The *manapua* lady's tinkling bell and the tofu man's plaintive call of "Tofu, *aburage*. Tofu, *aburage*." And it's a no-school day. That Saturday I was pumped up to go.

After a while the Lahaina bus turned down Main Street and came into view. It was packed with people and all kinds of goods.

Vegetables, mangoes, and even chickens tied up by the wings and kneeling down. Everybody who was waiting started to push and shove and this fat lady cut in front and pushed me aside like I wasn't there. Her eyes were so far away from her feet that she probably had no awareness of what was going on down below. By the time I got to the head of the line there were only two *nasubis* left. "Oh, well. You can't trust Yoshchan." I could already see the disappointment in my mother's face.

Everybody wears Saturday clothes on Saturday. But you can tell the locals from the country people because the country people wear *ho'okano,* dressy clothes. This lady was definitely from the country because she wore a hat and fancy shoes and carried a large *kalakoa* bag. She seemed to be looking for someone. And she was walking straight toward me.

She was strangely exotic and strutted like the peacocks in the plantation manager's yard. She wore a bright *holokū* and walked like she owned the street. She swished by me, and the heavy smell of gardenia perfume enveloped me.

Just then, her bracelet fell off, but she kept on walking. As soon as I picked it up I was thinking, "Did she notice? Is she watching?" Since I couldn't muster up the guts to figure it out, I ran after her.

"Hey, lady! Hey! Ah, . . . you drop this?"

She turned abruptly and swept me with her eyes. "Well, sonny. My. My. For goodness sake. Thank you."

With a swoop, she deftly took the bracelet with one hand and held me with her other before I could withdraw mine. Again her heavy perfume descended on me. I felt woozy.

"Listen, sonny boy," she said, "do you know where Mr. Ambrose lives?"

I was befuddled and was doing my best to regain my composure. Meanwhile, inside of my head I was thinking, "Yeah, I know him, but nobody calls Mu'umu'u 'Mr. Ambrose,' and my name is not 'sonny.'"

Out loud, though, I found myself saying, "Mr. Ambrose? The ditch-man?"

Her head was nodding.

I should have shook my head and said, "No, I don't know."

Instead I found myself nodding just like her. "Yeah, I know where."

"Where?"

She had me nailed. I might as well have been handcuffed.

Still I tried, "He lives far away, you know."

Even as I said that, I knew it wasn't going to work and I was going to be late for the ball game at Mill Camp. I was scared shitless but I found myself walking in the general direction of Piʻihana Camp. Toward Muʻumuʻu's house. It was going to be a strange day for me.

I'll never forget the first time I saw Muʻumuʻu. We were coming home from school when Joe asked, "Hey, you guys saw the man over there? He no more one hand."

"What you mean, 'no more one hand'?"

"No more."

"For real?"

"Let's go see!"

"No, you cannot just go look. He get one mean temper and a wild dog. But I tell you what. I show you guys how. You guys know how you make side eye?"

"What that, side eye?"

"Like this."

We all made side eye, but Joe said Jukichi didn't know how. "Come here, Jukichi. Stand by this mirror."

Standing there by the Coca Cola machine, Jukichi learned how to turn his eyes but not his head.

"Okay, you guys, no screw up now. I mean it. Muʻumuʻu is one wild man and his dog is worse. Follow me."

Joe put his finger to his lips, turned, and circled the block so that we could go by Mu'umu'u again.

We did okay at first, but were so nervous we almost peed in our pants as we walked toward Mu'umu'u. But then Hippo began to giggle. And Jukichi forgot how to make side eye and began to weave down the narrow sidewalk. He stumbled and stepped on the tail of Mu'umu'u's dog. Then all hell broke loose. The dog barked and started chasing us. Joe was running hard and yelling, "Look out for Mu'umu'u!"

We ran so hard we beat the dog to the gate of the churchyard and slammed it shut. Then with Mu'umu'u cursing us kids we took off across the graveyard and took refuge in the garage.

Joe kept on saying, "You stupid bastard, Jukichi. You almost got us killed!" He slapped Jukichi on the head and we all sat down to catch our breath. Then Joe told us how Mu'umu'u lost his hand.

In the old days they built an irrigation system to bring water from East Maui to tap the Haleakalā watershed. Working their way through the mountains, the powder-men used dynamite to blast out tunnels.

These powder-men were special and different from the ordinary *dokata*-men who worked with picks and shovels. They were the ones who started the powder fishing. They threw dynamite into the water and after the big "boom," the fish would belly up and be easily picked up. They said that Mu'umu'u was number one at powder fishing and was even able to get *akule* sometimes. Joe said the trick was to be able to spot the fish as they swam around, and Mu'umu'u was the best.

The way the powder part works is that you "see" the fish, then light the stick of dynamite and throw it just in front of the school and blow them up.

Joe whispered to us that one day Mu'umu'u waited too

long for the fish. . . . "Kaboom!" That was the story. After the accident, Muʻumuʻu was given the job of ditch-man. Everybody called him ditch-man up front, but Muʻumuʻu behind his back. His dogs were known to bite kids, and we weren't supposed to stare at his stump hidden in the sleeve of his chambray shirt. Everybody wondered what the stump looked like, but nobody knew. That was the Muʻumuʻu secret.

Just as Joe got finished telling us about Muʻumuʻu, the priest drove into the garage. Before we could escape, he asked us what we were doing there, and stupid Jukichi blurts, "Oh, we hiding from Muʻumuʻu."

"Hiding? Why?"

We couldn't believe it. Jukichi got all scared of the old priest and started to tell him everything. Soon we were in the rectory and the old priest was saying, "You boys did a real bad thing. God would want you to go to Muʻumuʻu right now and confess to him and apologize."

We all shook our heads. Who the hell would like to go back and talk to Muʻumuʻu?

"Well, then you must do penance. I want you all to close your eyes and pray with me and ask for God's forgiveness. And next Saturday morning early I want you all back here to help clean the yard."

As soon as we were out of earshot of the old priest, Jukichi got his head slapped for the second time. I thought Joe was going to kill him. What the hell did he have to tell the priest for? Just because he was wearing black clothes you don't have to tell him everything. "Jesus!"

By the time Saturday rolled around we had forgotten about the clean-up. That is, all of us except Jukichi. He showed up, and when his father found out about what he was up to, he gave him spankings.

But not long after, Jimmy got bit by his own dog. Bessie

had never bitten anyone before, but almost as if there was a curse on us, she bit Jimmy's hand and he had to have stitches and all. And it was the right hand, just like Mu'umu'u's!

Then another guy who was with us that day, Hippo, got an infection from a cut in his right hand, and Joe started to tell us that there was a curse on our heads because we didn't confess and do our penance. It was spooky. We were being cursed. One by one.

When Joe got his hand slammed in the car door, I became the only one left. But nothing happened to me—or so I thought.

Up close the country lady seemed more likable and less teacher-like. She had a pheasant lei in her *lau hala* hat, and her dress and exotic perfume all fit together. I couldn't quite figure out if she was a fun-lady or a mean boss-lady or what exactly had got me into nodding and going along with her.

By the time we reached the patch of tobacco growing near Camp One, she was sweating and her perfume was reeking and I felt like I couldn't breathe very well. I had tried three different versions in my mind of getting out of this, but each time I turned to look at her I knew it would be futile to try anything. So we kept on going. Past the chicken coop where I picked up a long feather that a fighting cock had lost from his tail, and over the hill toward the next camp.

Mu'umu'u's dogs were a wild bunch, and when they got excited—well, they always got excited—they barked up a storm.

Soon I saw the mango tree by the mill, and as we neared Mu'umu'u's house I began a serious search for a stick to ward off the dogs. But before I could find anything, the geese let the dogs know we were coming and the wild barking began. I was reaching for some rocks to throw at them when the lady walked right up to them and said, "Here, doggie . . . " and they started to act like puppies.

Holy moly. Is this magic?

"Tony! Tony?" she called. Then, "Anthony?" The door opened and Muʻumuʻu appeared. He looked disheveled, like we had woken him up, and instead of his usual faded chambray shirt with an empty sleeve, he was wearing a sleeveless undershirt. His stump was hanging out!

Had she not called out, if she had asked me if this was where Mr. Ambrose lived, I could have made my move. I could have said, "That's his house," and took off. Things were happening too fast for me.

Muʻumuʻu said, "Aunty!" and ran up to her. He picked up her bag, and she took hold of me, and before I could catch my breath we were in Muʻumuʻu's house. It was very neat and clean inside. The yard was a mess, but the house was washed-down spotless from being hosed down and wet mopped. There were the usual Catholic figurines hanging from the wall. Just inside the front door, leaning on the wall, was a twelve-gauge shotgun.

They were happy as hell. "Tony, I haven't seen you in three years."

"Really? That long."

I tried to collect my wits, and waited for the conversation to break and said, "I gotta go." My voice sounded funny. She would have none of it and pushed me down on a chair at the table. She searched in her bag and pulled out a well-laundered flour bag that was full of fixings for a lunch. The *pao doce* had that yeasty, sweet smell of just coming out of a stone oven, and she wouldn't listen to my plea that I had to go to the ball game.

Chewing on the bread, I watched her playing with her bracelets. It was spooky. She had a way of doing a twist with her fingers and wrist, and was dropping them on the table one by one. Right in front of me.

Then she gathered them up and slipped them back on her

wrist. Just when I figured that she had deliberately "lost" one of them to seduce me into helping her, I looked up at her and she stared right back at me and did that twist drop, twist drop again. She was not only a witch, she was showing off her witchcraft to me. I was getting woozy again.

All along I had the feeling that I didn't belong where I was. Up close to Mu'umu'u with his stump hanging out right in front of me. This uneasy feeling kept getting worse, so I made several attempts to leave, but after the third try she made me feel like if I asked again she would be stomping mad.

She pulled out some old photographs and started telling me about how young Tony had come to Maui with his mom and dad from Portugal and how his mom died when his sister was born and how his dad died when he got kicked in the head by a mule.

She saw how jumpy I was, and so she reached over into her *kalakoa* bag and said, "Here, I want you to take this home to your mommy." It was a neatly woven basket made of coconut fronds.

I opened the cover and on the bottom I saw the Lahaina *nasubis*, all neatly lined up. I started to count them. Ten, eleven, twelve, thirteen. Thirteen *nasubis!* Now I knew she was a witch.

I was sitting right in front of Mu'umu'u, and his stump was pointing at me. I tried desperately not to look at it. But the more I tried not to look the more it followed me. Even when I looked away it followed me.

When he tore a piece of bread with both his "hands," I thought I lost it. The moment passed but I thought I heard myself gasp. Afterward I could not tell if a sound came out from my throat. I hoped nobody heard me if I did gasp. I looked toward the door and all I could see was the shotgun.

They kept on talking, but I was so scared I couldn't make

out what the conversation was about. I couldn't hear a word and I was choking from stuffing my mouth with bread.

Finally what I dreaded most happened. He was beckoning me. "Come sit by me."

And she was nodding her head again. Up and down, up and down.

I found myself standing and shuffling toward him.

"You like see this?" The stump was inches from me! And he was saying, "Go ahead touch if you like."

I was chicken skinned to the tip of my toes. Shaking, I looked up at his face.

He was smiling. "Try touch."

I reached up and it was warm, supple, and smooth. "WOW!"

George Fujita is an emeritus retired staff psychologist at the University of Hawaiʻi-Mānoa. Born and raised in Wailuku, Maui, he lives in Honolulu with his wife, Pam, and their dog, Buddy. "Muʻumuʻu" is the Grand Prize Winner in the 1997 story competition.

On a calm moonlit night in Kapahulu, eleven-year-old Jay Agustin awakens to the sound of footsteps. The next night he wakes again and thinks he sees something. On the third night he meets the . . .

Woman in White

At the time I lived in Kapahulu, it was more like the country than a big city. Most of the streets were lined with unpaved sidewalks, and when the sun went down in the evening, cars on the road were almost nonexistent. The lot on which our house stood was occupied by four houses all lined in a row. We lived in the second house, which was obscured from the street by the first house. Not more than thirty feet away was the third house, a two-story house with the second floor built so that it overhung the side of the first floor. It made a convenient walkway that led to the fourth house.

The bedroom I shared with my older brother wasn't very large, so we had a bunk bed. I slept on the top bunk. This allowed me to see directly out the window. I slept facing the window, and since there was no curtain, I could see sunlight as well as moonlight occasionally shine through.

I was eleven years old when I experienced the scariest night of my life. Since it was a school night, I had gone to sleep by nine o'clock. I'm not sure what time it was when I suddenly awoke. Only the darkness gave me a hint that it was still nighttime. As I lay in bed, I could see the moonlight illuminating the second floor of the third house. For no better reason than curiosity, I scrambled to the window and looked out into the night. I could clearly see the house next door and could even see past the walkway to the fourth house. As I stared out, I thought I heard footsteps. I listened closely, but did not hear them again. The night was so still I did not even hear leaves on the trees rustling.

The next night, I again went to bed around nine o'clock. Again I woke up in the middle of the night. As I had the night before, I scrambled to the foot of the bed and looked out the window. This time, I thought I saw someone or something by the fourth house. I rubbed my eyes to get a better view, but nothing was there.

The following night I went to bed wondering if, almost wishing, I would be getting up in the middle of the night again. I got my wish; I did wake up. I quickly moved to look out the window. As on the other nights, the moonlight was bright enough for me to see the house next door, the walkway, and the fourth house. Unlike on the previous nights, however, I saw something that I will never in my entire life forget. In the walkway lay a woman on her stomach. She had long, stringy black hair and was dressed in a white gown. She was looking up, with one arm outstretched toward me. It appeared as if she was calling to me. By the look on her face, she appeared to be in pain. In the moonlight, her hair looked wet and the gown looked stained. Dark streaks ran down her arm, as if she were bleeding. Although to my young eyes she appeared old, she may have been about thirty years old.

I did not have to clear my eyes this time, for I knew my eyes were not playing tricks and it was not my imagination. Fortunately, I was not so frozen with fear that I wasn't able to quickly lie back on my bed and cover myself with my blanket. I prayed that she would not come any closer and look into my window. I kept wishing it would be daytime.

I woke up that morning with a start. I wondered about what I saw that night. No matter how many times I tried to convince myself it was a dream, I knew it was real. Throughout that day I wished night would not come. When

I went to sleep that night, I knew if I awoke in the middle of the night I would not look out the window.

My fears were for nothing. I did not wake up until it was daylight. In fact, after that night I no longer woke up in the middle of the night.

I still wonder sometimes who she might have been and what caused me to see her. One thing is for certain: no one can convince me that ghosts do not exist. Whenever I mention this incident, skeptics say it's the work of an overactive imagination. But their doubts don't bother me, for I know what I saw that night and I will never forget it.

Jay Agustin is a medical technologist at Diagnostic Laboratory Services/Accupath. Born and raised in Honolulu, he is a graduate of McKinley High School and the University of Hawai'i-Mānoa. "Woman in White" was awarded an Honorable Mention in the 1997 story competition.

Once in a while on certain hot days in old Lahaina, people see a Hawaiian warrior in the West Maui Mountains standing watch over the island. I have never seen him, but Asheley Kahahane tells about the day she saw . . .

The Sandalwood Warrior

I have lived in Lahaina all my life. I have never seen ghosts before until one day. My cousin Angela and I went to Kahului with my Aunty Momi to go shopping for food and other things. On the way back to Lahaina we passed the Tropical Plantation and my cousin and I started getting goose bumps like we were being watched by someone in the mountains. So my cousin and I looked up to the Sandalwood Golf Course and we saw a warrior with thick, muscled legs and a nice brown helmet. I think he was as tall as the banyan tree down at Front Street.

The next day I called my cousin and asked her, "Angela, did you tell your mom about the thing we saw yesterday?"

"Yes," she said, "I did tell her about it. She told me that the thing we saw was just an old warrior watching out for anybody who harms his land."

Twelve-year-old Asheley Kahahane enjoys true scary stories because she likes to be scared. She maintains that her Aunty Maile tells such good scary stories that it is hard for her to sleep at night. Besides listening to scary stories, Asheley plays volleyball or spends time talking with friends on the phone. She lives in Lahaina with her parents and brother and sister.

Three figures of white vapor suddenly appear in a young girl's bedroom one night. A large hairy hand grabs her wrist on another night. Her father says it's all a bad dream, but she knows the true story of . . .

Hickam Ghosts

I was six years old when it happened. The year was 1959. We had moved into the new Hickam housing complex on Fox Boulevard. It was a nice, two-story townhouse with three bedrooms and one bathroom. My sister and I shared one bedroom.

One warm summer night I had been sleeping soundly on the bottom bunk. Suddenly, I felt a bitter chill around me. I opened my eyes and looked around.

Standing at the side of my bed were three illuminated figures. They had no features at all. They looked like human silhouettes made up of white vapor.

Being from a devout Catholic family, I believed the cross pendant that I wore around my neck would protect me from harm. It was blessed by the parish priest with holy water. I lifted the pendant toward them. It didn't work. They were still there by my bed.

The taller figure moved toward me. I could feel the air getting colder around my neck, and then I felt pressure around my neck. He was trying to choke me! I tried to bring my right hand up to make the Sign of the Cross. In my fright, my hand felt like it weighed a ton. I watched my hand move in slow motion. At the same time I was finding it difficult to breathe.

I managed to make the Sign of the Cross. I began to recite The Lord's Prayer. "Our Father, who art in heaven, hallowed be thy name. Thy kingdom come, thy will be done . . . "

They disappeared. The room was warm again. I was afraid to move. I stayed frozen in my bed.

"Mommy, Mommy, Mommy!" I cried.

"My dad turned on the hallway light and checked on me.

"What's the matter?" he asked.

"There were three ghosts, and they tried to choke my neck," I told him frantically.

He looked around as if to find some clue. He turned to me and replied. "There's nothing here. You had a bad dream. It's all right now. Go back to sleep."

My sister and I switched beds several months later. I slept on the top bunk. One night I woke up because my nose was running. The tissue box was on the right side of my bed against the wall. I reached over to get a tissue.

Suddenly, a large hairy hand came up from behind the tissue box and grabbed my wrist. I felt a surging scream coming up my throat, but only a small squeak came out. A cold chill ran through my whole little body.

I tried to pull free. It was a grip as strong as a man's. I pulled the hand and arm toward me and opened my mouth to bite it. It disappeared.

Once more I called my mom. Once more, Dad came. This time he told me it was a cockroach. My dad doesn't believe in those things, I figured.

After that scary incident, my mom called the priest. She had the priest bless every inch of the house including the closets. I never had another scare again.

Later, my mom told me that some of the other residents in the area had sighted ghosts in their homes too. So I wasn't dreaming after all. But even now I won't keep a tissue box anywhere near my bed.

Maureen Trevenen was born in Honolulu and lived at Hickam Air Force Base from age four to age eleven. After military assignments in the Philippines and Arizona, her family returned to Hawai'i, where Maureen graduated from Radford High. She spent seven years on the mainland (where she survived two tornadoes, a flood, and the Three Mile Island disaster), and is now back in Hawai'i to stay. Married, she has three daughters and a grandson.

Laupāhoehoe
Beach Park

On the Big Island's Hāmākua Coast, this tongue of black lava that sticks out into the blue Pacific holds a grim reminder of nature's fury. In 1946, a tidal wave swept across the village that once stood on this lava leaf (that's what *laupāhoehoe* means) peninsula and claimed the lives of twenty children and four teachers. A memorial today recalls the tragedy in this pretty little beach park where the land ends in black sea stacks that remind me of tombstones. When the wind is in the trees you can hear the voices of the lost children.

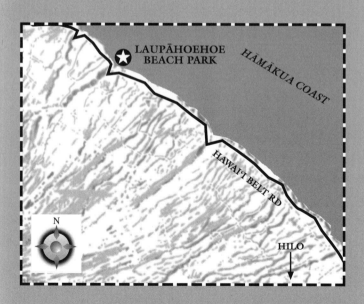

Family

···

Immigrants came to Hawai'i seeking fortune, opportunity and a better way of life. As years went by, their colorful stories were passed from generation to generation. From the days between the second and the third generation, Richard S. Fukushima recalls the story of . . .

Mamoru

K enneth Mamoru Tanigawa lived a very simple life with his parents on the island of Kaua'i. His parents were plantation workers who worked for the pineapple cannery.

Mamoru-kun, as his parents called him, always enjoyed listening to stories his father heard at work from Native Hawaiians. The stories Mamoru liked best were ghost stories, which the Japanese called "obake."

Mamoru's mother used to teach him the Japanese beliefs about doing things correctly. She used to remind Mamoru that if he did something incorrectly, something would happen to him. One of the things Mamoru recalled was his mother telling him: "If you sleep with your hands upon your chest, you will have bad dreams." Mamoru, of course, did not believe it.

After Mamoru finished high school, he left home and went on to the university, but the stories his father told and the beliefs his mother taught remained in his subconscious. Mamoru studied hard and tried to better himself, because his parents had high aspirations for him. Upon graduation, he entered military service and served a tour of duty in Japan.

Mamoru enjoyed Japan, He was in the land of his grandparents. He traveled the country and visited as many places as he could. After a year, Mamoru received a telegram from the American Red Cross. His father was seriously ill, and Mamoru was granted emergency leave to fly home to Hawai'i.

Mamoru was then placed on a C-120 military aircraft that flew from Japan to Wake Island, the first leg of the long trip back to Hawai'i, which took ten hours of flying time.

At Wake Island, there was a five-hour stopover. The crew of the aircraft, Mamoru, and another serviceman from Hawai'i who was also going home on emergency leave were billeted in the barracks for the five hours. Everyone took a nap after the long, exhausting flight from Japan.

Suddenly, Mamoru was awakened by a loud, strange noise telling him that his father was dead. Mamoru couldn't believe it, so he jumped up from the bed and looked around the room and saw that everyone was sleeping. Where did the voice come from and how did the voice know that Mamoru's father was dead? It puzzled Mamoru and he wanted to call home to Hawai'i from Wake Island to see if it was true. He found a telephone, but then decided not to call. He decided to wait until he reached Honolulu.

Five hours later, the crew was back on the airplane heading for Hawai'i from Wake Island. This trip was another ten-hour trip. Approaching Hawai'i, the plane flew over the island of Kaua'i. Looking out the window, Mamoru saw an unusual ring of clouds covering the island. Only the mountaintop could be seen from the plane.

When the plane landed at the Honolulu Airport, Mamoru called his sister to pick him up. She told him that their father died. Mamoru asked what time, and learned that his father died at about the same time he heard the voice on Wake Island. However, Mamoru still could not believe it. The next day he flew back home to Kaua'i for the funeral.

The day of the wake, Mamoru went with his family to the mortuary to bring his father's body home. Following the hearse from the mortuary, Mamoru saw his father's face in the rear window of the hearse. He did not tell anyone, fearing that no one would believe him.

"Yes, Dad," he silently told himself, "I have come home to see you. May your soul rest in peace."

Richard S. Fukushima was born and raised on Kaua'i. He attended the University of Hawai'i and Kaua'i Community College and served in the United States Army and the Hawai'i Army National Guard. He currently works at the Hanapēpē Public Library. A widower, he enjoys golf, bowling, fishing, cooking, quilting, and writing poetry and short articles.

Surfers in Hawai'i will tell
you that once in a while they
feel that something or
someone is in the water
beside them—a dark
shadow in the clear sea.
Most of the time it's only their
imagination, but in this case it
turns out to be . . .

The Ghost Who Surfs

On Maui, there's a beach named D. T. Fleming. It's upward of Nāpili east of Kapalua side. On one beautiful morning, Thursday, November 15, 1989, I met a surfer named Adam Nahele. He is five feet six inches tall, with black hair and brown skin. He is twenty-eight years old and surfs almost every day.

He told me he was surfing around six or seven in the morning with his longboard. He said the waves were high, that it was seven to eight feet. He said he caught around twenty-four waves that day.

But something was wrong when he was surfing that day. He felt a ghost spirit by him. He was about to catch a wave when he saw a ghost beside him. The ghost was surfing with a longboard and wore gray short pants. He was about five foot six and looked like he weighed around 150. He had black hair, brown skin, and black eyes.

Adam's eyes popped out. He caught the wave and took it back to shore. He was still scared when he got to shore.

When he looked back, nothing was there. Everything disappeared like the smoke of a cigarette. But Adam was still scared until he got home and figured it out.

He didn't find a clue until he closed his eyes and tried to take a good look at the face. He looked harder and knew that it was his father from the dead. Adam was proud of what happened in his life that day. He knew it was going to happen one day to him. Adam told me his father came back to check his surfing skills.

Twelve-year-old Hapa Koloi enjoys playing football and basketball. Born in Honolulu, Hapa was raised in Lahaina, where he now resides with his parents and four sisters. He enjoys listening to the stories of his father, Sefita, writing original poems about his life, and reading biblical stories.

Honokahua
Burial Site

Discovery of bones on a sand dune overlooking
Honokahua Bay and the subsequent public out-
cry by Native Hawaiians forced developers to
halt construction of The Ritz Carlton Kapalua on
13.6 prime oceanfront acres in 1987.

Today, the burial site is *kapu*, reserved for
Native Hawaiian ceremonial and religious practices. It is a State Historic Place.

The developer relocated the hotel uphill and
inland, away from the burial site where the
remains of 1,029 Hawaiians, dating between AD
850 and the early 1800s, now rest in peace.

After dark on moonlit nights many people,
not just Hawaiians, sense an uncommon presence
here.

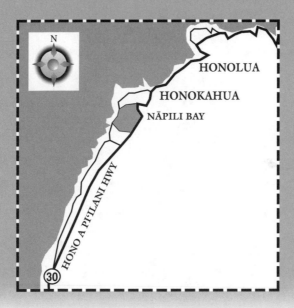

In the summer of 1853, an eighteen-year-old carpenter named Abraham Hussey stepped off a sailing ship and went ashore at Waipi'o Valley on the Big Island of Hawai'i. Several generations later, a young Hawaiian woman visiting Nantucket discovers an eerie link to . . .

The Saltbox House

By the time I reached thirty-seven years of age, I was possessed with the desire to own a home of my own. I madly clipped dream houses out of *House Beautiful* and *House and Garden* magazines. Then I'd drop them into a wish file that from time to time I'd look at wistfully.

One day I spread out the photographs of my fantasy home— the one my heart longed for, the home that would make everything in my life fall neatly into a blissful space.

A close friend looked at the photographs and remarked at how similar they all were, even though they had been clipped from several different sources over a period of many months. The house I longed for and was driven to have was basically a saltbox design with weathered clapboard shingles on the sides, a two-story house with windows that let in the morning sun.

It was during this time that another friend and I planned a vacation to New England to see the leaves change color and hunt for early American bric-a-brac. The trip included a side jaunt to Nantucket, which by then would have been deserted by the summer crowds. Besides, Nantucket was the home, I told him, of an ancestor of mine.

We arrived by ferry on the island in the early afternoon and quickly found a charming bed-and-breakfast inn. The next morning I awoke refreshed in a canopied four-poster bed and looked out my upstairs window. My heart stood still.

There was my house. The house of my dreams. The house I'd clipped dozens of times and stored lovingly in my manila folder. It was the house I'd longed for.

The morning sun streamed through its multipaned front windows and bathed the bright red geraniums in the window boxes in a warm, crisp glow.

I threw on my clothes and raced downstairs into the hallway and out into the cobblestoned street. Within seconds I was across the street standing in front of the saltbox house, my heart pounding.

Like all the older homes built in Nantucket during the prosperous whaling days of the early 1800s, the house bore a sign with the name of the family that had occupied it at the time, and a medallion of authenticity.

I stood looking at the name on the housefront in shock. It said: "Hussey."

How could it have been just a coincidence that I was Abraham Hussey's great-great-granddaughter? Was it some strange ancestral memory that had made me long for the saltbox house? Long to go home again? Who knows.

Kaui Goring Philpotts is a freelance writer, author and former food editor of the *Honolulu Advertiser*. Educated at the Kamehameha Schools and University of Oregon, she worked in radio, then for many years as a columnist and lifestyle feature editor at *The Maui News*. She is the author of *Maui Cooks* and *Maui Cooks Again* and *Great Chefs of Hawaii*, a companion book to the Discovery Channel series. She is currently working on *Hawaiian Country Tables*, a collection of vintage island folk recipes from 1930 -1950.

Pi'ilanihale

For generations Hawaiian elders have warned everyone to stay away from Pi'ilanihale on the Hāna coast. It is still considered *kapu* by many. A national historic landmark, little known or visited by anyone but Hawaiians, this sixty-acre compound is the largest royal residence on Maui, perhaps all of Hawai'i.

Here King Pi'ilani, the first king of Maui, lived in the sixteenth century on a bluff overlooking the Pacific. Pi'ilani, who died about AD 1500, is noted in Hawaiian traditions as the first king of all Maui.

Such a commanding site, archaeologists say, indicates it probably was a *luakini*, or war *heiau*, and a place of human sacrifice. Archaeologists say the site includes a massive five-story stone temple 174 meters long and 89 meters wide. The site includes a large grove of *'ulu* (breadfruit).

Abandoned after Kamehameha's death in 1819, the *heiau*, marked by coconut trees, almost disappeared under jungle growth. "The first time I went up there, oh, it was chicken skin," said Francis "Blue" Lono, a descendant of Pi'ilani, who is *kahu* of the *heiau*. "I told my father, 'I get funny feeling at the *heiau*,' and he said, 'It's natural, it's just family.'"

The *heiau* dominates the 122-acre Kahanu Garden, now tended by the National Tropical Botanical Garden.

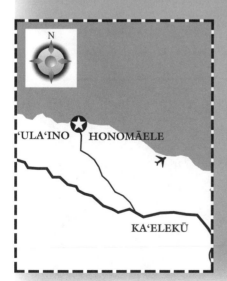

While visiting her family's summer home on the Big Island of Hawai'i, a Maunawili School student is reunited with an ancestral spirit in . . .

Great-Grandpa's Ghost

In 1994 I stayed in Laupāhoehoe on the Big Island in my grandma and grandpa's summer house that my aunty, uncle, and cousin just moved into. One night at midnight when the house was all quiet, I heard a noise and I thought that it was just the wind. But then I heard it again and again. I went to my cousin's room.

"Jake, I can sleep in your room tonight?"

"Fine den," he said.

Then I heard the same noise again and again. "Jake, you heard that?"

"Yeah," he said.

Then we went to his parents' room. We told them what happened. Then me and my cousin got up and started to eat something.

So then out of nowhere this figure came out of my great-grandpa's picture.

"It's Grandpa Kanoa!"

Then me and my cousin got all freaked out and screamed for about two minutes. Since we had the key for my Grandma Kanoa's house, we went inside and woke her up and then we told her what happened.

The next day we got a priest to bless the house. We thought that it wasn't safe. But the priest said, "It is safe or your money back."

Then we were all laughing except me and Jake. I didn't want to sleep at my aunty's house the next night or ever again.

Jerrica Ann Keanuhea Lum was only ten years old when she wrote about her visit to Laupāhoehoe. She is now a fifth-grade student at Maunawili Elementary School. Born on January 13, 1987, Jerrica is the daughter of Arnold and Jerri Lum. She has an older brother and two sisters. Her hobbies are writing, dancing hula, and playing the piano.

1900-1950

A skeptic pooh-poohs old Hawaiian ways around a campfire on Mauna Kea one night, and a sudden breeze becomes a hard wind that mysteriously douses . . .

Mauna Kea Campfire

When I was stationed on the Big Island in 1945, I always tried to visit local places of interest. I loved the legends and had a great deal of respect for them and the other customs and practices of the people of these islands. Whenever a group of us went to visit special places, we were briefed on the proper respect due, and to the best of my memory, most of us conformed

One weekend in September, after the war was over, a group of us were given permission to climb Mauna Kea. Two of our group were experienced climbers. In fact, they had climbed Mont Blanc. There were eleven of us, both men and women. I was a WAVE. We were all stationed at the Naval Air Station in Hilo. Hilo back then, or for that matter the entire Big Island, looked nothing like it looks today. It was a quiet place. The war really made a difference on that island. It was a very somber place in my recollections.

We left the base in the rear of a truck, eager for our adventure. It was a beautiful day—warm in Hilo, gradually getting colder as we went up the mountain. We stopped at a *puka* to practice. We all did well on that test. Then we got back in the truck and continued up the mountain.

We reached an altitude of nine thousand or ten thousand feet, where there was a shelter. At that spot, before unpacking our gear, we were given a little talk. We were told to stay away from any of the caves, pits, and mounds we might encounter on our hike up the mountain. It was explained that these might be burial caves, and must not be disturbed. Someone also informed us of the legends of the "marching soldiers" that have been seen in this area.

A couple of the men started a wonderful campfire. We ate our hot dogs, and we even had marshmallows. After eating, we started singing, playing games, and sharing tales. Most of the talk was, of course, about being back home. After a while the conversations changed to the experiences we were having here in Hawai'i.

The fire was keeping us warm, and consequently the "talk story" continued. Several of us expressed our appreciation of these islands, and especially our desire to uphold the ancient traditions. Most agreed, but there was one dissenting voice. He informed us that he had no time for old traditions. He thought they were all based upon fear tactics designed to keep people in line. In fact, he informed us that he had entered many areas that were *kapu.*

It is hard for me to explain what happened in the next few minutes. He had no sooner finished his last sentence when a very cold stirring of air began to engulf us. In fact, the breeze turned into a cold wind. The fire, which had been a roaring inferno, suddenly went out. There were of course sounds of disbelief when this occurred. We tried to talk ourselves into thinking it was just a natural happening that occurs on the side of a mountain.

After this incident, there was some debate as to whether or not we should continue our climb up the mountain. We did. However, because of the altitude, and because we were amateurs, only two reached the top. I might add that the man who was disrespectful did not attempt the climb. I think the experience of the lost fire got to him more than to the rest of us. We only ended up remembering the "goose bumps," and having even more respect for those things that have no logical explanation.

Alberta Lindsay, who lives on the Big Island, served in the WAVES during World War II and was one of the first women assigned to Navy 24 in Hilo. After the war, she returned to her native Pennsylvania and received a B.S. in nutrition. As a nutritionist for a nonprofit organization, she worked on radio and television with Ed McMahon and Dick Clark. She later earned an M.A. in guidance and counseling and an Ed. D. in administration, and worked as a teacher, guidance counselor, psychologist, and school administrator. She and her husband of forty-four years have a son and a daughter. "The Mauna Kea Campfire" was awarded an Honorable Mention in the 1997 story competition.

RON TERRY

The Ghost in Mauna Kea

By day, the summit of Mauna Kea is as colorful and inviting as a Wyland painting. Above are sapphire skies, while below—an odd delight—is a white carpet of clouds. The red and yellow cinder cones protrude from this fluffy deck like underwater islands.

The observatories appear to float in the rarefied atmosphere, glistening whales of silver and white. When it snows, skiers and snowboarders in Day-Glo outfits school like reef fish on the slopes. Unseen below the cinders are more wonders. The *wēkiu* bug scavenges lava crevices for wind-blown morsels, protected by its unique biology from the nightly deep freeze. Every day the mountain absorbs the dry air and then "exhales" it at night, moistened and expanded by residual heat from the dormant volcano.

As night falls, colors fade from pastels to gray to black. When you are alone on the mountain in a darkness full of infinite stars, the bone-chilling cold brings new power to old stories. Here, Pele engaged in earth-shaking rivalries with her sisters, Hiʻiaka and Poliahu, the goddesses of lightning and snow.

The telescope operators pass busy nights in sealed domes. Inside fortresses of wires and gears, they reduce stars to images on a computer terminal and numbers on a printout. It is easy to forget the real stars hidden by the thin metal skin above them. If they venture outside and linger in the cold, Mauna Kea seems lonely and forbidding, even to a scientist. The summit is no place for mortals.

Sometimes things happen. Operators report that pale shadows appear suddenly, only to dart behind the round corner of a 'scope before they can really focus. Everyone says it's just disorientation brought on by altitude and cold. Occasionally, they hear the soft rattle of an *ʻulīʻulī*—but it could just as well be the incessant wind blowing bits of plastic around on the cinders.

A road to the summit was first scoured out in 1964. Those

were the days before environmental impact statements, when archaeology happened accidentally, at the end of a bulldozer blade. There are no official reports, of course, only rumors, but bones of more than one skeleton were disturbed by all the roads and pads and domes that have enthroned the observatories as the modern kings of the mountain.

Such an unearthing—the unhappy bones of an *ali'i*, whose people took such trouble to bring him here—might explain the small manifestations of another presence. What mournful chant of death and renewal accompanied these processions of bones?

Observatory operators and astronomers come and go, highly paid international migrant workers. But a few have spent decades on the mountain. Again and again they have visited the observatories and ventured into the night. Some of them have seen and heard more than pale glows and gentle rattles. Those are little things, not worth much more than a night's worth of gentle teasing from colleagues. Other incidents are more disturbing—and these are reported only in whispers.

When over and over you see the sharp flash of flame in a crack in the cinders, you begin to realize there is something more than *wēkiu* bugs, something more than bones, under you.

The deep, hoarse whispers emanating from below belong to a power greater than trapped air—or even a disenchanted ghost. The great sighing lungs, the giant glowing heart—these reveal the true presence under the cinders.

Death is not final for a goddess. She may rise again, brought to life by the renewed faith of her people. It will not be well to be atop cold Mauna Kea when she awakens.

Ron Terry, Ph.D., is an environmental impact consultant and part-time faculty at the University of Hawai'i at Hilo. Born in San Diego, he has lived on the Big Island since age twenty. As a student doing meteorology research he spent many nights on Mauna Kea. He now prefers to research—and slumber—at sea level. "The Ghost in Mauna Kea" was awarded an Honorable Mention in the 1997 story competition.

You must always be prepared for strange encounters on Lāna'i. The island is full of mystery, superstition and surprising revelations, as Helen Fujie explains in two chilling stories. In the first, a young boy is entrusted with a sacred vision from ancient Hawai'i.

Katsup

In the early 1920s, when Lāna'i City was being built around what is now Dole Park, a naughty boy named Katsuto Fujie was sent from Lahaina to stay with his oldest sister and her husband, James T. Sawada, who was the "carpenter boss" of a crew of construction workers from Japan.

Since his sister was busy as a nurse's aide at the hospital and his brother-in-law was too involved in the building of all the plantation houses, the nine-year-old "Katsup" was left alone to fend for himself, especially during the summer.

He roamed the hillside back of the "*haole* camp" where the Hawaiian Pineapple Company supervisors lived. He also went beyond the Kō'ele Ranch, where the Lodge at Kō'ele now stands. When he hiked higher and deeper on to Lāna'ihale, a vine-covered cave revealed to him a beautifully carved canoe with its oars, and in the canoe were some calabash bowls and a feather cape and a helmet.

He was so awed he did not dare touch them. He ran down the hill to the Rev. Daniel Kaopuiki and told him about the cave and its contents.

The Reverend Kaopuiki wanted to see the place and the sacred things for himself, so the two went back to the hillside, but they couldn't find the cave at all.

Then the Reverend Kaopuiki said that "Katsup" was trusted and blessed by the spirits of the Hawaiians to receive a vision of perhaps the burial cave of a chief. Or perhaps it was King Kamehameha I's treasure trove, because the king used to enjoy his summers on Lāna'i at his Kaunolū house site far downhill to the south.

A retired school teacher and administrator, Helen Fujie writes regularly for the *Lanai Times* and occasionally for the *Honolulu Advertiser*. Born and raised in Kahului, Maui, she is a graduate of the University of Hawai'i College of Education. She taught on Lāna'i for forty years and worked as a substitute teacher and volunteer until 1996. Married to Roy K. Fujie since 1944, she and her husband have three sons and two granddaughters. "Katsup" is from a collection, "Lāna'i Visions," which was awarded an Honorable Mention in the 1997 story competition.

Kaunolū Village

Out on Lāna'i's nearly vertical Gibraltar-like sea cliffs is an old royal compound believed to have been inhabited by King Kamehameha the Great two hundred years ago. Now a national historic landmark and one of Hawai'i's most treasured ruins, the village of Kaunolū includes eighty-six house platforms and Halulu *heiau*, an imposing three-tiered rock altar named for a mythical man-eating bird. The village may yet yield the bones of King Kamehameha, whose burial site to this day is known only to the moon and the stars.

When you visit Kaunolū you can—if you dare—search for the lost fish idol of Kunihi, a three-foot stone with a crudely carved face and arms that once stood on the altar of Halulu.

In 1921, archaeologist Kenneth Emory learned that Ohua, the last man living in these parts, was told by King Kamehameha V in 1868 to hide the fish idol, but he mishandled the idol and died.

The stone fish idol of Kunihi was last seen in 1921, Emory said, "lying face down not more than a hundred yards up the gulch from the altar and against the west bank."

If you find it, call 911. I wouldn't touch it, either.

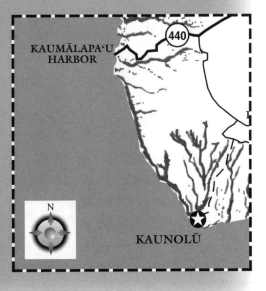

The second encounter on
Lāna'i involves a vision of
artifacts from a different era.

Cowboy Kauwenaole

Ountime night in the late 1930s when Cowboy Kauwenaole (Elaine Kaopuiki's father) was out in the eerie moonscape of the Garden of the Gods for a round-up of stray cattle that had scattered from the Kō'ele Ranch area, he noticed a strange fragrance. There were no flowers anywhere near, and, anyway, it didn't smell like the local plumeria, *pīkake*, or *pakalana*, but more like an English or New England lavender cologne or perfume. He followed his nose to a hole in the ground among all those dark rock formations.

To his great surprise he saw a well-lit opening that revealed a beautiful candle-lit bedroom with a lace-covered four-poster bed. He ran back to let the other cowboys know of his discovery.

But when they all followed him to the spot, they couldn't find the underground room in the middle of the night in the middle of the Garden of the Gods. So they teased Kauwenaole about having a nightmare vision.

A retired school teacher and administrator, Helen Fujie writes regularly for the *Lanai Times* and occasionally for the *Honolulu Advertiser*. Born and raised in Kahului, Maui, she is a graduate of the University of Hawai'i College of Education. She taught on Lāna'i for forty years and worked as a substitute teacher and volunteer until 1996. Married to Roy K. Fujie since 1944, she and her husband have three sons and two granddaughters. "Cowboy" is from a collection, "Lāna'i Visions," which was awarded an Honorable Mention in the 1997 story competition.

In old Hilo town three generations ago, the Japanese grocer Sanzuchi Kaneshige encounters the spirits of Chinese workers who died building a bridge across a swift river.

Hitodama

My grandparents, who were immigrants from Japan, operated a small general store outside of Hilo soon after the turn of the century. One day, my grandfather went to town on his horse-drawn carriage.

By the time he finished the business in town, it was already quite dark. As he was hurriedly making his way home, his horse suddenly stopped and neighed as if frightened by something in the middle of a tall wooden bridge. Try as he might, he could not make his horse move.

This was a bridge that spanned a deep gorge and a swift river. He had heard that, many years prior to this, Chinese immigrant laborers had slaved under dire circumstances to build this bridge. He had heard that many laborers had lost their lives in the process of building this bridge. This was the infamous bridge built by the sweat and tears of early Chinese immigrants.

Just as he was remembering this story told to him by the old-timers, there suddenly appeared before him several eerie bluish-colored balls of fire floating in the air around him. He knew that these must be the *hitodama*, or balls of dead sprits, that he had heard of before.

Although he was almost frightened out of his wits, he closed his eyes tightly and managed to recite over and over again the Buddhist incantation "Namu Amida Butsu, Namu Amida Butsu, Namu Amida Butsu" ("Hail Amida Buddha, Hail Amida

Buddha, Hail Amida Buddha").

Although it seemed like an eternity, he prayed and recited the incantation for only five to ten minutes. Finally, when he slowly and fearfully opened his eyes, the *hitodama* had disappeared without a trace. At the same time, the horse slowly started to walk forward again.

In this way, my grandfather was released from the stranglehold of the dead spirits and managed to safely return home to his wife and his many little children, including my father.

I believe that, more than the divine intervention of Amida Buddha or the power of the incantation, the thing that perhaps ultimately pacified the dead spirits was the compassion and the sympathy my grandfather, also an immigrant, felt toward the dead who died unfulfilled and angry at not being able to make the long-sought American dream come true.

Not too long after this incident, my grandfather closed down his store and moved to the North Shore of Oʻahu with his growing family. After all, as the head of the household his primary responsibility was the safety of his family.

Gladys Kaneshige Nakahara is working toward a Ph.D. in Japanese literature while teaching Japanese language full-time at the University of Hawaiʻi at Mānoa. Born an American citizen in Japan, she came to Hawaiʻi to attend the University of Hawaiʻi. She and her husband, Earl, have three children. "*Hitodama*" was awarded an Honorable Mention in the 1997 story competition.

Ship and Shore

··

When you go on a sea cruise in the Hawaiian Islands aboard the SS *Independence*, you may encounter more than you bargained for, especially if you book a cabin . . .

Down At C Deck Aft

In the early '80s, the SS *Independence* had a rainbow painted along the passageways and in the cabins. The rainbow ran all the way, port and starboard from bow to stern. It ran through every cabin in every level on every deck. It was quite a sight, part of the Hawaiian theme in those days, I guess.

The ship went into dry dock for a major overhaul. I forget which year it was exactly, but you could find it in the ship's log.

There was a worker whose job it was during dry dock to paint the rainbow in and out of every room of every deck. A big, boring labor-intensive job. There's a lot of jobs like that on ships.

They say this guy was not hitting on all cylinders. He was just kind of a wiper, I guess you'd call him. That's like the lowest class you can get at sea—someone who paints and polishes the brass and wipes everything down every day. It's an endless task.

Anyway, one morning after he'd done the all-night shift, he just disappeared. The yeoman looked for him and couldn't find him. Finally, they had a call from someone who reported hearing a whole lot of noise, someone screaming, in one of the last cabins down at C deck aft. So the yeoman went down to investigate and found the cabin door was locked and they couldn't get it open.

When they broke through the door, they found this guy sitting quietly in the middle of the room. He had painted the entire room red. It was just dripping down the wall and he was totally out of his mind, babbling and delirious.

They took him off the ship and put him in a mental institution, just locked him up. Two weeks later, he requested that a priest come and see him, and one did. About two or three days after the priest came, the guy committed suicide.

Well, the yeoman had the room repainted and fixed it up and that was that—or so they thought. The captain took the ship back to Honolulu to return to service. On the morning of the first day of sailing from Aloha Tower, the inaugural sail out of Honolulu with passengers still boarding the ship, someone heard a lot of yelling from C deck aft—that same cabin all the way aft.

The yeoman got the key and opened the door and the noise stopped. In the middle of the room was a priest performing an exorcism. Everyone just stood there, surprised. When the priest finished, he picked up his stuff and never said a word. He just smiled and left, walked down the gangway and disappeared.

And this is odd: nobody who stood watch at the gangway could remember having seen a priest come aboard. Nobody, not the captain or anyone, had sent for a priest. Nobody recalled ever seeing the priest until they discovered him in the cabin. He just appeared, did his thing and left. How he knew about the incident and even which cabin to exorcise is still a mystery.

None of this ever made the news, and as time went by and crews came and went, the story gradually faded from everyone's memory. Only a few people who have been with the company a long time even know about the incident down at C deck aft. I learned about it from Captain Zarnoff, who was first mate back then.

That cabin's still there on the ship today and you could book it for a cruise, I guess, if you wanted to—but rumor has it, it's not real comfortable.

Eugene Le Beaux is a former Los Angeles jazz musician who played gigs in New York, Paris, and New Orleans before he came to Hawai'i in 1988. A trombone player and master of the conch shell, Le Beaux went to sea aboard the SS *Monterey* as the cruise ship's band leader and played Big Band era music, jazz, rock, and Broadway tunes until the *Monterey* went out of service. For the past decade, Le Beaux has performed aboard the SS *Independence* cruise ship, which makes weekly interisland voyages in the Hawaiian Island chain.

Sometimes a fisherman hooks into something bigger than *ulua*, as Bernard D. Gomes discovers when he moves rocks in the path to his favorite Big Island fishing spot on a . . .

Bad-Luck Weekend

My two neighbors, Shane and Wayne, and I decided to go fishing at my favorite spot in Ka'ū. Another friend, Al, was to meet us at the entrance at two o'clock in the afternoon. By the time we got there, it was four o'clock. Al was not there. We looked for tire tracks or any other traces he might have left to let us know that he had gone to the shore. We didn't find any. We wanted to beat the sunset, so we moved some rocks that were blocking the path and drove through and replaced the rocks. We still had between an hour and a half and two hours of off-road terrain to cover to reach the spot.

We were about a quarter mile down the shore from my spot when darkness fell. We decided to camp by a large black sand hill. We got our fishing poles and lanterns and started to fish. It was a slow fish-biting night. So about 1:30 in the morning, Shane and I decided to kick back at the camp.

After about an hour had gone by, I heard my camper door open. I turned and looked out my camper's side window and saw a man holding a plastic bag with what looked like blue glow beads in it. The bag blocked part of his face. Thinking he was one of my friends, I said, "Hey, you getting your secret stash ready?" When I got no reply, I stood up and looked. The camper door was still open, but the person was gone.

Shane was fast asleep by his truck. I saw a flashlight beam coming toward me. It was Wayne. He said, "Bernard, look at my lantern." I saw the glass was missing and the housing was all twisted. Wayne said, "I placed the lantern on a bank behind me and started to fish. All of a sudden I saw my lantern fly over my back and head."

I couldn't figure it out. The wind would knock it down, not fly it over. Plus, the wind was almost as calm as before a storm. The water was calm, and Wayne was dry, so it wasn't a wave. And to his back was the bank of the sand hill.

I had to ask him if he had been back to the camp earlier, and he said no. So I told him about our visitor, and we both looked at each other and nothing more was said.

Morning came, and we decided to move the additional quarter mile to the area we had planned to go to in the first place. When we got there we made up camp and started to catch bait for the *ulua* poles and sail line. I baited the sail line with seven hooks. I checked it about three hours later and found all seven leaders cut. I replaced the lines and rebaited and sent the sail out again. We saw a large wave coming in and called to warn each other. Our bait bucket was in the water, and the rope that was tied in a bulletproof knot from the bucket to a spike untied itself in front of our very eyes. The bucket slowly floated away.

We caught some more fish and placed them in a tidal pool. A few hours passed and we checked the sail line. All the leaders were cut again. This time we decided not to try it again. Whatever was out there was not meant to be caught.

Only one strike, a forty-pounder, was all we caught. The bites came to a standstill that night. Not all the *palu* and chum we used brought them back.

The next day we packed up and headed to Hilo about noon. Right after lunch, as we were heading out, I heard a high-pitched, metal-to-metal rubbing. I got out of my truck and saw that the cab and camper were butted together. I looked underneath and saw two cracks on both sides of the truck frame. So the camper and cab were all that was keeping the truck together. Knowing this, I had to drive very slowly. By the time we came to the main paved road it was nine at night.

No gas stations or stores were open. Heading to Hilo, my friend's truck ran out of fuel at Volcano. So when we got to Hilo, we got some gas and had to go back to Volcano, fill up his truck and then drive back to Hilo.

By the way, my friend Al never showed up. His wife told me he had a heart attack the night before he was to meet us. (He's doing fine.)

This is one fishing trip my neighbors and I will never forget.

Bernard Gomes is a mechanic with Yamada and Sons in Hilo. He enjoys fishing, exploring old Hawaiian ruins, listening to Hawaiian music, and reading, listening to, and writing stories about Hawai'i.

While paddling her kayak down Kaua'i's Nā Pali Coast to the remote Kalalau Valley two days after Hurricane 'Iniki, a woman adventurer discovers the truth about herself and nature in . . .

Spirit Winds

"You must leave early from Kalalau—real early—if you want to miss the wind on the paddle back to Kēʻē." Everybody knew it.

"Early" means dark in Kalalau—dark sky, dark water, dark stillness. It is an impulse in the pre-dawn hours, an inner sense when intuition tells you: "now," and you nose the boat into the shadow of a swell, blades pressed against the still night air.

The day we left the valley, it was just past "early." I knew it, and so did Jan. The wind was on its way.

"Feel it?"

I nodded. It wasn't more than a brush, a light pressure on my cheek, but I knew. "Wind's starting already."

"Sky's light."

"Yes, we missed it."

A little too late on rising, and an unexpected delay in loading the boats had cost us needed time. I looked up the coast. My mind flashed back to the valley beach, less than a week ago: the false morning calm, the alarm sent, the gathering wind, and the gusts that met us aloft in the chopper, only hours before ʻIniki hit.

"Ready to go?" Jan's voice brought me back to the damp sand beach at Kalalau. I paused, and looked back up the coast.

"Go now," a quiet voice said.

"Now?" I asked my inner guide in silence. "Still now?"

"Go."

I eased the boat over an oncoming swell, and slid into the seat. I knew better than to argue with the wisdom and good intentions of my higher guides. But I couldn't help asking: "No lessons, no tests?"

I could feel their amusement.

"You're safe," the answer came. "Go now."

I pulled hard on the right and nosed the boat up-coast. Jan met me a few hundred yards into the paddle.

"Okay?" she asked.

"What do your guides say?"

"They say go," she replied.

"So do mine. Let's paddle."

We pulled on ahead of the lower beach. I glanced back at the valley. We had spent the last two days sorting, cleaning, and repacking gear left by anxious campers on the morning of 'Iniki. With help from another team, we packed three loads into medic 'copters for the flight back to Hanalei. The storm had spared our cave and the boats we had left there—paddles still tucked beneath the hull.

The day of the storm and the aftermath were full of adventure and near escapes: the branch that fell just past the van, a house we avoided that later collapsed, the inner voice that sped us through a maze of hotel common rooms to rest in a private suite. When the storm hit, I was in the suite, deep inside a yoga pose. Wind swirled past the hotel, tugging at my thoughts, beating against the calm I sought within.

Where else do you go in the midst of chaos? I had asked. "Deep inside," the inner voice affirmed, "into the moment and the task at hand."

And afterward? "You open, and align." The words of my teacher and friend, Barbara Mahaffey, rang through the following days of aftermath. "Open to your truth and higher guidance."

Barbara was a therapist and healer from Scottsdale, Arizona, who had introduced me to my guides. "Truth," I had learned from her, was a heightened energetic state, a state of awareness and clarity. It flows through your actions, thoughts, and deeds when you access and open your upper chakras—energy vortices that connect the human form and its energy field with universal health and healing vibrations. I knew the upper energy points, and kept them open as best I could: one above the head to the earth, one above that to the spirit realm, and one, four feet above my head, that opened into universal energy and the wisdom of my celestial guides.

"Open up, and your awareness heightens," Barbara said. "Your emotions clear. You 'see' from a higher perspective."

You are also safe, I discovered, and centered, even in the midst of screaming winds.

"Still coming up," Jan called over the freshening breeze as we passed the valley peaks. I stared into the fetch of open sea.

I nodded. "Better relax," I replied, "we have a long paddle ahead." Long ago, I had learned not to fight with nature.

Half an hour passed. I was pressing harder, pulling more, bending low. I pulled hard to hold my ground in a sudden gust. What wind is this, I wondered. The trades, Mālua Kele? Lanikuʻuwaʻa, the wind of Kalalau? I thought of names I'd heard among the island chants. This wind, too, must have a name. It was not wild, like 'Iniki, but still steady, strong, and building. It was a force to be reckoned with.

I paddled on. Gusts gave way to a strong, persistent push. Something has to give, I thought. More gusts came. The pressure increased. I softened my gaze, and dropped back into my body. How do you slip through the wind, I wondered. How do you soften enough so the air streams through you? Where do you ground in the surface chops?

"Go high," the inner voice explained.

"Go in," it said. I softened my gaze once more and

dropped back into that calm familiar place within my body. From here I began to explore the tension. Another gust grabbed the upper blade. I gripped the paddle harder.

"Breathe." The voice was gentle but firm. "Release your upper shoulder. Shorten your stroke, and relax."

I was not afraid. After years of yoga and outdoor adventure, I knew what my body could do. I took a long slow breath and went back inside. I pressed my buttocks into the seat, released the spine forward, opened the chest, and shortened my stroke. For the next hour I followed the movement and release of my muscles, working the body from the inside out in a long slow yoga pose. My breath remained steady and slow. My awareness grew, and embraced the outer and inner world of the paddle. Streams of ocean air dragged past me. I lowered and lengthened into the wind, both in and out of the body. Mindful and alert, yet centered and relaxed.

Jan paddled ahead of me as we worked our way up the coast. She too had gone inside, deep in an hour-long "asana" that began when the last gust hit us. We kept paddling. There was no stopping now. No outer place to rest.

I thought of Barbara. Years ago at sunset we had kayaked part of the Kona coast en route to our beachfront camping spot. It was her first time out. The wind came up unexpectedly, pushing her back. I slowed to match her pace. Time sped past us as we inched along. Twilight darkened around us. Then Barbara veered off toward shore. Jan and I watched in amazement as Barbara paddled to the beach through a narrow break in the rocks. She landed like a pro and stepped out onto the cobbled berm.

"My guides said to go," she later said. "So I went. I knew I would make it."

That was the first time I really knew what she meant, the first time I started to trust my guides. And I knew we would make it then and now. I caught up with Jan half a mile below

Hanakāpī'ai beach. We still had a ways to go, and the wind kept building. More asana, more breathing. But I knew we were both starting to tire.

I dug my paddle deep into the chop. "Look," I said aloud in a gentle voice to my guides. "I don't want to do this alone. Please help."

"Open," they reminded me.

I drew my focus upward, to a point in the wind four feet above my head. I felt the familiar release, like a breath letting go. Energy flowed down through me.

"Now ask."

I asked again for help. Energy flowed through my arms. My thoughts cleared, my body relaxed, and I began to paddle with an easy, fluid stroke, despite the push of the wind. I looked up, and around me, into the sunny world beyond my paddle tips. I began to enjoy the trip, and the flow that carried me well past Hanakāpī'ai, past Kē'ē beach and onto the beach at Hā'ena.

The landing was wet and tumbled, but it flowed too. The boat flipped in the plunging surf. I swam to shore and ran for the boat. Jan was already there. We laughed as I dragged the kayak up the beach. I was not out of breath, and not the least bit tired. I could still feel the warm clear opening above my head.

Later, we sat on the beach over hot tea and humor, reliving the morning's trip. The wind still blew hard past the breakers, heading down-coast toward Kalalau. I leaned back into the air streams. The energy of the morning still flowed through my arms. No aches, no tired muscles, just a sense of lightness and well-being.

"What a magical trip," Jan said.

I smiled, and thought of a passage I'd read only a week before. My guides could have written it: "Magic is a human experience. We will perceive it if we are totally intuitive, act with instinct-like impulse and realize how the forces stream into us without any personal effort."

Catherine Chandler, M.S., has been leading health and adventure retreats throughout the islands for the past five years, guiding others into a deeper, more intuitive feel for nature as a sentient, healing presence in their lives. For her, Kalalau is a valley steeped in magic; and the sea, a place of mastery and self-discovery. She lives among the wind and healing waters of North Kohala on the island of Hawai'i.

Kaulu o Laka Heiau

On Kaua'i's North Shore beyond Hanalei, on a knoll above the boulders of Kē'ē Beach, stands a sacred altar of rocks, often draped with flower leis and ti leaf offerings.

Dedicated to Laka, the goddess of hula, this altar may seem like a primal relic, but it is very much in use today. Dancers of Hawai'i's *hula hālau* (schools) come bearing gifts of flowers. Sometimes, mothers place the umbilical cord of newborns here in a revival of old Hawaiian ways, once banned by missionaries.

In Hawaiian myths, Lohi'au, a handsome chief, danced here before the fire goddess Pele, and their passion became Hā'ena, which means "the heat."

Unusual incidents are often reported at this very spiritual Hawaiian place. I always feel a little uneasy here-—as if something out of the ordinary may suddenly occur.

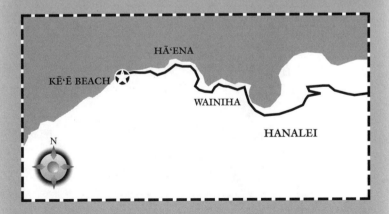

On an interisland ship bound for Maui, a humming sound breaks the silence of a calm, dark night and a strange apparition appears in the 'Alenuihāhā Channel. Many passengers aboard the *La'anui* are convinced they are seeing . . .

The Ghost Fleet of Kamehameha I

Perhaps in February or March of the year 1864, the brig *La'anui* was in the channel between Maui and Hawai'i, the channel called 'Alenuihāhā. This was a calm but dark night. Calmness spread over the shining surface of the water. The ship rolled this way and that while some passengers slept and others remained awake with the mates.

It was at or near midnight when those who were awake exclaimed as they saw two ships approaching toward their stern. These were large ships; one had no sail, as her masts were all broken, and the other had only a single mast. She had only a foresail. The two ships pitched and tossed as though in a great storm.

To those on board the brig *La'anui*, it seemed that a strong gale came along with them and angry billows threatened to overwhelm them. They appeared to sink and at times to rise higher than the tip of the *La'anui*'s mast. The passengers of the *La'anui* cried out in awe. "Such strange ships. What a mysterious sight." Goose pimples rose on every one on board and some actually cried.

Children were seen landing at the cliff without looking back in their dread at the loud voices of their parents from the sea. From the battered ships were heard the screams of prisoners, shouting, lamentations and so forth. The ships did not come too close but remained some distance away.

One of the ships was toward the port side of the brig *La'anui*, and the other on the starboard side. The *La'anui* stood becalmed, with the prow moving this way and that for lack of breeze.

O readers who read this, forgive your writer and this tale, because I know that it will remind you of friends, kinfolk and close relatives who were swallowed into the deep bowels of the ocean on one of our missing ships. So the writer begs your pardon for stirring up your grief, O readers of this mysterious and somewhat sad tale.

The one thing that greatly puzzled the passengers of the *La'anui* was that she did not rise and fall and only the two ships, that they were looking at, did so. All these actions of the ships struck terror to all those on board the *La'anui*.

This apparition of the battered ships was seen for about three or four hours. It ended by their changing into a white cloud which spread over the surface of the sea and vanished. Not long after they had seen this the passengers of the *La'anui* began to discuss it among themselves. They were eager for the arrival of daylight but very soon they heard a humming sound in the calm stillness. It was strange for such a sound to appear on a calm sea and it sounded to them like the noise made by a school of fish suddenly startled at the sight of man. So did it sound on this night on which a calm reigned.

The people peered this way and that and noticed a fleet of canoes being vigorously paddled. They seemed to be heading toward Maui, because all of the prows pointed toward Hāna.

There were a great number of canoes, both single and double. A high platform on a double canoe could be distinctly seen by them all and they guessed that probably a chief occupied it. There were about six double canoes and hundreds of single ones being paddled along. They guessed that these canoes they were observing were war canoes, hurrying to reach land before the first light of day arrived.

Perhaps this was the ghostly company of Pai'ea (Kamehameha I) on the way to war against Kahekili on the famous battleground of 'Īao, known as Ke-pani-wai (dammed water) and Ka-ua'u-pali (clawed cliff).

Perhaps the readers will be surprised at this and say that it is not true, for their fleets of canoes do not appear as apparitions. The story does not say so, but one can recognize the fact that not only the canoes appeared but everything else, even to the men that manned them—all were in the ghostly company.

The men who manned the canoes had large physiques, from those on the double to those on the single ones. The passengers also noticed a large, dark object coming from a distance. When it drew near they saw double canoes, and those on board were easily distinguished, such as the paddlers, the carriers of the taboo stick and the occupants of the platform.

Among them was a very large man sitting in the midst of some people, which looked to be a council of war for the battle to be fought the next day. They guessed that the large man was not the yellow-shelled *'a'ama* crab whose claws were broken off (meaning a weakling) but Pai'ea (Kamehameha I) himself. The large man wore a long feather cloak and a high-crested helmet on his head. His kindly eyes looked from under his brows with a smile at the log-like *La'anui*, standing by, becalmed. The others on the platform with him looked angrily toward us, and perhaps we were saved because of the large man. Those who looked at us with unfriendly expressions sat with him as though they were his foster sons, friends and war leaders.

The reason we saw every one so plainly was that we had three lighted lanterns filled with whale oil hanging on the rigging and up where the ropes were attached to the mast. The bright lights were aided by the perfect calm. The passengers hid in the dark to watch.

After the fleet of canoes had passed on, the passengers of the *La'anui* knew that these belonged to people long dead and they were filled with fear and great dread. They sat in silence, not uttering a sound, wondering whether their lives were safe, because they had heard that ghosts were makers of mischief.

Mary Kawena Pukui (1895-1986) began collecting proverbs, riddles and poetic expressions on the Big Island of Hawai'i when she was fifteen. She is the principal author of the *Hawaiian Dictionary*, *Place Names of Hawaii*, and *'Ōlelo No'eau*, a treasury of Hawaiian sayings. In a fifty-year association with the Bishop Museum, she translated thousands of Hawai'i's legends, chants, and ghost stories, including this excerpt from "Seeing Thousands of Ghosts for a Single Night at Leilono, Hawaii," which appeared in *Holumua*, January 14, 1893. It is reprinted here with the permission of the Bishop Museum.

The Guide to Spooky Places

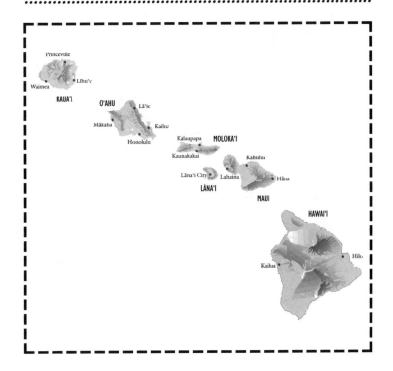

The Guide to Spooky Places

Hawai'i is full of "chicken skin" places—places of power, mystery, spiritual and natural beauty that will make you shiver in the tropic heat.

You can experience chicken skin on all islands by visiting *heiau* (temples), petroglyph fields, monuments and memorials, or by seeing natural phenomena like a night rainbow or red-hot lava trickling underfoot or by experiencing the eerie silence of the rain forest.

Some people get chicken skin atop 10,023-foot Haleakalā crater watching the sun rise, or deep inside the Thurston lava tube, or underwater, when they encounter a white-tipped reef shark.

A walk in O'ahu Cemetery at sunset will give you a chill. So will a visit to Moloka'i's Mo'omomi Dunes, which yield prehistoric skeletons of flightless birds and sometimes even human bones.

Don't be afraid to take pork over the Pali or take one of Madame Pele's lava rocks from the Big Island. Every school kid in Hawai'i knows those are only old wives' tales meant to scare tourists. Although old folks still have lingering doubts.

You can experience chicken skin at any time, but sunrise and sunset are ideal, especially if you are all by yourself.

I personally have experienced chicken skin while walking on red-hot lava as it ran into the sea near Kamoamoa one night, while observing a night rainbow on Maui at Māʻalea Bay, while tracing my finger in the stone petroglyphs at Puakō on the Big Island's Kohala Coast, while wandering, alone, in the half-light of Wao Kele O Puna rain forest and while hearing chants at sundown at Pohukaina Mound near ʻIolani Palace.

Each island has many hair-raising places, but I think the Big Island, with its live volcano, the largest concentration of petroglyphs in the Pacific, and the biggest sacrificial *heiau*, is Hawaiʻi's chicken skin capital.

One caveat about *kapu* before you go: In Hawaiʻi *kapu* is more than a "no trespassing" sign. *Kapu* today is backed by a state law that makes it a crime to violate sacred places. There's a $10,000-a-day fine if you disturb human burials. Of course, that's the very least that could happen to you if you mess with old Hawaiian bones.

Now, the first guide to Hawaiʻi's spooky places.

Princeville
Waimea • Līhuʻe
KAUAʻI

Kauaʻi

Kaulu o Laka Heiau *(See page 155.)*

Kaʻawakō Heiau, Waiʻaleʻale

You can only see it from a helicopter if you're lucky and the clouds part. I have only seen it once. On the nearly mile-high summit of Waiʻaleʻale, the wettest spot on earth, is a ten-foot-square rock *heiau* known as Kaʻawakō. That's Hawaiian for "the kava drawn along," a reference to the flood of water in this lofty place where 360 inches of rain a year is common. Hawaiians may have thanked the gods for rain or prayed that it stop. Either way, Waiʻaleʻale, which means "rippling or overflowing water," was sacred to early Hawaiians, who built terraces, house platforms and temples on its summit.

At the turn of the century men on donkeys took several days to reach the summit and check the rain gauge. Today, a helicopter hovers over a tiny peak while a daring weatherman jumps out to check the gauge before clouds engulf the summit. A scary job. Go on a clear day, otherwise all you will see is the inside of a cloud.

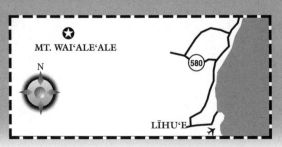

MT. WAIʻALEʻALE

N

580

LĪHUʻE

O'ahu

Pohukaina Mound *(See page 72.)*

Ulupō Heiau *(See page 33.)*

Pu'uomahuka Heiau

On O'ahu's North Shore on a bluff overlooking the world's most famous surf stands Pu'uom-ahuka ("hill of escape") Heiau, which always gives me chicken skin.

Here, in 1794, three of Capt. George Vancouver's men were sacrificed. Here, in 1819, the year before missionaries arrived, King Kamehameha II ordered all idols destroyed. Yet this *heiau*, the largest on O'ahu, often shows signs of contemporary worship. You may see small sacrifices of ti leaf and stone, fruit and flowers. You may even have the feeling, like I do, of being watched.

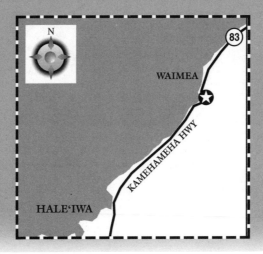

Royal Mausoleum *(See page 35.)*

Kaʻena Point

Kaʻena is a needle-like peninsula that points due west toward the setting sun over the Pacific. This spectacular finger of lava at the foot of Kuaokalā Ridge also pointed the way for ancient Hawaiian souls of the dead who took a flying leap (*leina*) into the spirit (*ʻuhane*) world.

Each island has a *leina a ka ʻuhane*, but Oʻahu's is singularly impressive because of its edgy, end-of-the-world setting. Waves sweep in from opposite directions on Kaʻena Point, where you can see both north and south shores of Oʻahu.

Offshore, low, jagged rocks are pounded by waves. One large, flat rock, Pōhaku o Kauaʻi, was pulled over from Kauaʻi by the demigod Māui to bring the islands closer.

Don't go near the water here, or rip tides may carry you to the other world via Tahiti.

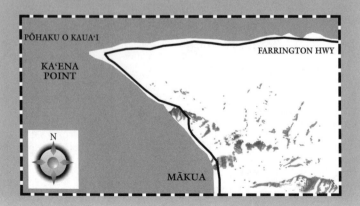

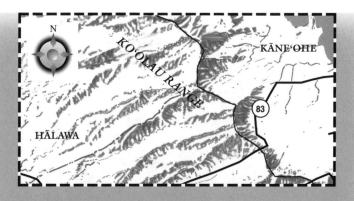

Hālawa Valley

A mysterious valley of temples, Hālawa Valley has been off-limits for centuries. Now the controversial $1.37-billion H-3 interstate freeway slashes through the heart of one of Hawai'i's last largely unexplored ancient communities. One *heiau* after another stands along almost the entire route through the majestic Ko'olau range. And deep in the valley is another enigma of the Pacific: a complex of seventy-five *imu* pits—used for what? Mass sacrifice or major *lū'au*?

Motorists should be advised to watch out for strange sights and sounds. Like conch shells blowing in the wind. Or odd vapors that suddenly appear. When you drive through the valley, worry not that four 120-foot-long, 40-ton concrete girders supporting the freeway collapsed in the summer of 1996, for no apparent reason, injuring four carpenters. Do not be concerned that two construction workers died in an earlier mysterious incident after churning up bones (*iwi*) of ancient Hawaiians. Ignore the fact that a Hawaiian *kahuna* has placed a curse on the entire 16.1-mile freeway. And some folks still worry about taking pork over the Pali!

Moloka'i

Ili'ili'ōpae Heiau

Biggest, oldest and most famous *heiau* on Moloka'i, Ili'ili'ōpae is four tiers high and longer than a football field. The big rock temple attracted *kāhuna* from all islands who came to learn the rules of human sacrifice at this university of dark and sacred rites.

Contrary to Hollywood's version, historians say, victims here were always men, not young virgins, and they were strangled, not thrown into a volcano, while priests sat on *lau hala* mats watching silently. Spooky, eh?

Climb uphill to gain a sense of the immense size of this *heiau*, which overlooks four fishponds on Moloka'i's east end, near Mapulehu's historic mango groves.

Lāna'i

Garden of the Gods

Each time I set foot on Lāna'i I find myself inexplicably drawn to this desolate, windswept place. The Garden of the Gods is the ultimate rock garden—a rugged, beautiful, barren place full of rocks strewn by volcanic forces and honed by exposure to the elements to reveal an infinite variety of shapes and earth tones. Go at sunrise or sunset when the sun's rays cast strange shadows on the helter-skelter rocks. Or visit by the light of the full moon. If you dare.

GARDEN OF THE GODS

N

Kaunolū Village *(See page 133.)*

MAUI

Maui

Haleakalā Crater *(See page 53.)*

Honokahua Burial Site *(See page 115.)*

Pu'u Keka'a
The eighty-five-foot-high volcanic cliff that juts into the sea, dividing three-mile-long Kā'anapali Beach, is known by Hawaiians as a *leina a ke akua*, a place where spirits leap into eternal darkness.

Often called Black Rock, this site is now haunted by videocam-toting tourists who gather each night at sunset to watch a young Hawaiian runner, in traditional *malo*, carry a flaming torch to the cliff edge and swan dive into the sea—a leap reminiscent of old Hawaiian ways.

In a display of cultural bravado, the new Sheraton Maui has built luxury suites on Pu'u Keka'a, where souls check into the other world. Good night and sleep tight, *malihini*.

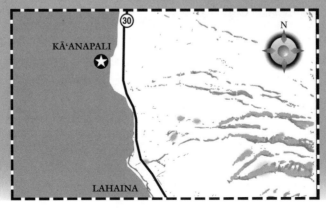

The Lost Island of Moku'ula

Six feet under a Lahaina softball field is one of my favorite chicken skin sites on Maui—the lost island of Hawai'i's little boy king. Here, more than a century ago, Prince Kauikeaolui lived with the love of his life, his sister, Princess Nahienaena, on a one-acre island, Moku'ula, set in a large freshwater fishpond. The little prince grew up and ascended the throne as King Kamehameha III when he was only ten.

Torn between love for her brother and the new Christian morality, Princess Nāhi'ena'ena grew despondent and died at the age of twenty-one. King Kamehameha III, who reigned twenty-nine years, longer than any other Hawaiian monarch, died in 1854. He was thirty-nine.

In 1918, the island and a royal tomb were covered with dirt to make a baseball diamond at what is now Malu'uluolele Park in Lahaina.

One of the most important historic sites in Hawai'i, the island was nearly forgotten until 1992, when archaeologists found relics on a preliminary dig. Even though the lost island is covered by tons of dirt, archaeologists and Hawaiians alike say something still radiates from this royal place. You may experience it yourself when you stand at home plate.

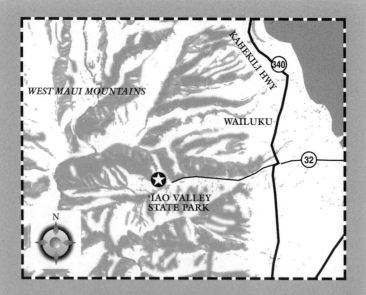

'Iao Valley State Park

Ancient Hawaiians named the valley 'Iao (literally Supreme Light) in honor of the supreme creator. It's easy to see why when misty clouds are backlighted by gold rays in the afternoon.

In 1790 King Kamehameha and his men engaged in the bloody battle of 'Iao Valley to gain control of Maui. When the battle ended, so many bodies blocked 'Iao Stream the battle site was named Kepaniwai—"damming of the waters."

Today, this peaceful valley, the eroded volcanic caldera of the West Maui Mountains, is a state park full of tropical plants, rainbows and waterfalls, swimming holes, hiking trails and 'Iao Needle, a 2,250-foot stone basaltic finger that looms out of the mist like the finger of a god.

Pi'ilanihale *(See page 119.)*

'Eke Crater

In the West Maui mountains stands a nearly mile-high flattop mountain that looks like it should be a landing zone for aliens.

A sugar loaf among spiky peaks, 'Eke Crater is the source of myths old and new. Hawaiians believed 'Eke is where survivors of the great flood at the beginning of time landed their canoe when the water receded. New Age disciples claim 'Eke is the landing zone of extraterrestrials.

Neither canoe nor spacecraft was in evidence the day I gazed upon 'Eke, but it's easy to see how such beliefs originate. The mysterious crater is extraordinary in shape and size and would be a singular attraction on Maui except that it's upstaged by high and mighty Haleakalā, more than twice its size.

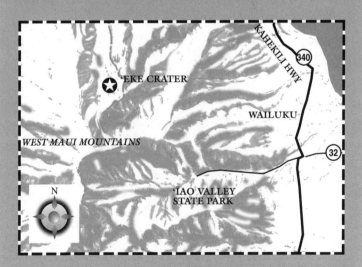

Big Island of Hawai'i

Pu'uhonua O Hōnaunau

With fierce, haunting idols, this sacred site on the black lava Kona Coast is foreboding. To ancient Hawaiians, however, it must have been a welcome sight, for Pu'uhonua O Hōnaunau served as a sixteenth-century place of refuge, providing sanctuary for defeated warriors and *kapu* violators.

A great rock wall—1,000 feet long, 10 feet high and 17 feet thick—defines the refuge where Hawaiians found safety.

Hale O Keawe Heiau holds bones of twenty-three Hawaiian chiefs. Other archaeological finds include burial sites, old trails, and an ancient village. You can see reconstructed thatched huts, canoes, and idols and feel the *mana* (power) of old Hawai'i.

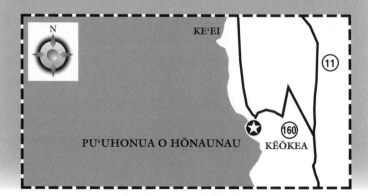

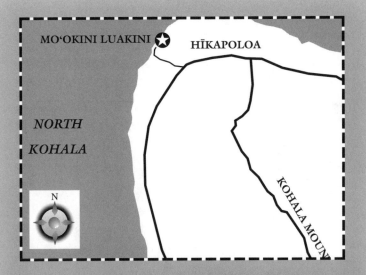

Mo‘okini Luakini

On the Kohala Coast, where King Kamehameha the Great was born, stands Hawai‘i's oldest, largest, most sacred religious site—the 1,500-year-old Mo‘okini Heiau.

Once used for human sacrifice, the massive three-story stone temple is dedicated to Kū, the Hawaiian god of war. It was erected in 480 A.D. under the direction of High Priest Kuamo‘o Mo‘okini. Each stone is said to have been passed hand-to-hand from Pololū Valley fourteen miles away by eighteen thousand men who worked sunset to sunrise.

King Kamehameha, born nearby under Halley's Comet, sought spiritual guidance here before embarking on his campaign to unite Hawai‘i as a kingdom. Go in late afternoon when the setting sun strikes the lava rock walls and creates a melancholy mood.

Kīlauea Volcano *(See page 13.)*

Waipiʻo Valley

Once the domain of kings who called it "the valley of the curving water," Waipiʻo Valley is a spiritual place haunted by all manner of creatures, like Nenewe, the Shark Man, who lives in a pool, and the ghost of the underworld, who often surfaces through a sea tunnel.

The 2,000-foot-high cliffs laced by 1,200-foot-high twin falls contain burial caves of Hawaiian chiefs. The valley is widely believed to be the final resting place of the *kāʻai*, the sennit caskets holding the bones of Hawaiian chiefs Līloa and Lonoikamakahiki, mysteriously reclaimed by Native Hawaiians from the Bishop Museum. After dark you may hear Night Marchers chant as they go.

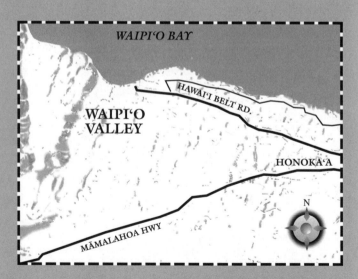